Spindles and the Mystery of the Missing Numbat

Spindles
& the Mystery of the Missing Numbat

• BARRY CHANT •

Tyndale House Publishers
Wheaton, Illinois

Other books in the Spindles series:
Spindles and the Giant Eagle Rescue

Library of Congress Catalog Card Number 90-71917
ISBN 0-8423-6213-4
Copyright © 1975 by Barry Chant
All rights reserved
Printed in the United States of America
99 98 97 96 95 94 93 92 91
9   8   7   6   5   4   3   2   1
Cover Illustration © by Ted Enik
Interior Illustrations by Lorraine Lewitzka

To Michael, who was never intentionally the model for Spindles, but whose lively personality seems to have rubbed off on Spindles, anyway.

CONTENTS

CHARACTERS

1. **Spindles**—Timothy Thornton, whose father and mother own the Dusty Range sheep station.
2. **Redgum**—A great eucalyptus tree, wise and strong.
3. **Gawk**—Spindles' emu friend.
4. **Hippie**—Spindles' educated emu friend.
5. **Tank**—A dinkum Aussie goanna.
6. **Roo**—A kind, motherly, gentle kangaroo.
7. **Joey**—Roo's joey.
8. **Bilby**—A spritely, rhyme-speaking desert bandicoot.
9. **Gloria**—Bilby's mate.
10. **Gleam**—A chattering, excitable, but helpful galah.
11. **Percival**—A lonely numbat.
12. **Lonely**—The station's quiet stockman.
13. **Sleepy**—Lonely's loyal dog.
14. **Kamulla**—An aboriginal station hand.
15. **Mr. & Mrs. Thornton**—Spindles' parents

HOMESTEAD
GRID
NUMBAT FOUND X HERE
OPAL POOL
BILBY'S HOME
CLIFFS
DUSTY RANGE
TRACK (3 MILES)
REDGUM
X
CAMPERS
JOEY FOUND HERE
CREEKBED

I

Spindles and the Christmas Stranger

Spindles was puzzled.

The whole station was buzzing with activity. Everyone was busy. For it was the day before Christmas, and preparations were in hand for the annual Christmas party.

Spindles liked Christmas—he always had. You couldn't help it really. Visitors, gifts, food, sweets, music, fun. It was a great time for children.

But now he was about your age, and old enough to think about important things, he was disturbed. Somewhere in the back of his mind, questions were beginning to take shape. Birthday parties were held in honour of someone's birthday. Wedding celebrations were only held when there was a wedding. But what about Christmas? Why did people hold Christmas parties? Strangely enough, no one had ever tried to explain it to him.

So Spindles was puzzled.

And he decided to ask someone about it.

He wandered about the station property looking for someone who might know. He drifted down past the woolshed and the sheepyards, kicking the red dust into miniature willy-willies as he slurred his feet along. His spindly legs seemed whiter than ever against the brown earth. In fact, this was why people called him Spindles. (His real name was Timothy Alexander Thornton.)

At the shearing shed, he met Butch, one of the stockmen. Years ago, when Butch first tried to shear, he had cut a couple of sheep.

"You oughter be a butcher, not a shearer!" someone had said. So "Butch" he became.

Actually, he was now a very good shearer, among other things, and he was permanently employed at the station where Spindles lived.

So Spindles decided to ask Butch about Christmas.

"Hey Butch," he demanded. "Why do people have Christmas parties?"

"G'day, Spindles," answered Butch. "Owyer goin'?" And he seemed as though he would walk off.

"G'day Butch," answered Spindles, realising that he should have said this first. Then, as he saw Butch about to make off, he spoke quickly again. "Hey, Butch! What about my question?"

"What question, Spindles?"

"Why do people have Christmas parties?"

"Well, now," said Butch thoughtfully, "Christmas parties. Well, you see, Spins, it's like this. You see, at Christmas time . . . Well, Christmas time, it's like . . . well, as far as I'm concerned, at Christmas all the shearin's over an' done an' it's a good time t'ave a bit of a break, and meet all the boys, an' like, well, celebrate."

This long speech seemed to have somewhat exhausted Butch, and he made to go on his way.

"But why is it called Christmas?" Spindles again demanded.

"Look, Spins," Butch replied, "I gotta go now. I'll see yer later on."

And with that he was gone.

Spindles leaned against the shed, sheltering from the Australian inland sun in the shade of the overhanging iron roof, and pondered Butch's explanation. It hadn't been very helpful, really.

So he drifted around the homestead buildings, wondering who else might help him. The kitchen seemed suddenly to be in front of him, so he spoke to Captain, the station cook. He was a jovial soul who obviously enjoyed both his work and his product. Spindles was always welcome in the kitchen, and could always be sure of a handout of some kind, even though his parents had given Captain strict instructions "never to give him anything to eat between meals."

"Well g'day, young feller," said Captain.

"'Day, Captain."

"You know you're not supposed to 'ave anythin' to eat between meals."

"Yes, I know," answered Spindles, grabbing a slice of cake and stuffing a large part of it into his mouth as he answered.

"Hey, Captain," he went on. "Why do we have Christmas parties?"

"Why do we 'ave Christmas parties? Well, everyone 'as Christmas parties, Spindles. We 'ave 'em like anyone else does."

"Why?"

The cook looked mildly annoyed. (Boys who keep on asking why can be a nuisance.)

"I told yer why, son."

"You didn't really," persisted Spindles. "Why does everyone have Christmas parties?"

"Because they do, that's why. As for me, Christmas is the one time in the year when I can really let me 'air down and turn on a slap-up feed. Then I can show people 'ow I really can cook. Turkey, roast spud, stuffing, cake, tidbits, Christmas pud—not to mention

my own special 'damper a la capitaine.'" (And when he said this, he used his own idea of French pronunciation and grammar. No French man would have understood it, but it sounded very impressive to Spindles.)

"Is that the only reason we have Christmas parties? What about places where they don't have special cooks?"

"Look, Spindles, I'm very busy getting things ready for the party tonight. Why don't you run along now, eh?"

So Spindles left the kitchen and headed for a clump of small gum trees about a hundred metres away. He sat down there in the shade and picked a small branch for brushing the flies off.

About half an hour later, he heard the sound of a motor bike, and he realised that Lonely, the boundary rider, was coming in for the party. Lonely never talked much to anyone. He spent all his time doing the rounds of the fences, checking them for holes and watching out for sheep that might be sick or injured.

In the old days he used to go out on horseback and stay out for days at a time. Now, with the motor bike, he could actually come home every night, but he rarely did. He still stayed out for as long as a week, cooking damper on a little camp fire, and boiling his tea in an old black, dented billy, that usually hung rattling on the back of the bike. Lonely always took his dog, Sleepy, with him. The dog rode in a box fitted where the passenger seat used to be.

Spindles stood up and wandered out to the middle of the track. Lonely slowed down and stopped. Sleepy, who was lying in the box, opened one eye, spotted the trees, jumped out, and sprawled in the shade, both eyes closed even before he was settled.

"G'day, Lonely."

"G'day, Spins."

There was silence for a while. Lonely was never in a hurry to speak.

"Lonely, can you answer a question?"

"Dunno, son. Ask me."

Encouraged, Spindles went on. "Lonely, why do we have Christmas parties?"

"Beats me, son," answered Lonely. "Yer dad always expects me to come in for 'em, but I'd just as soon stay out in the bush. Give me peace 'n' quiet any time. Can't stand all the noise an' carrying-on of Christmas parties. But I've sorter gotta be there."

"But why do we have them?"

"Blowed if I know, Spins. Can't stand 'em meself."

"But why do other people have them?"

"That's a good question, son."

And with that, he clicked the bike into gear, a sound which, although faint, was immediately heard by Sleepy, who stood, shook himself slightly, and sprang with surprising agility into his box, where he promptly lay down again. The bike took off, and Spindles was left alone.

It was nearly lunch time, so Spindles walked over to the homestead. On the way, he caught sight of Kamulla, an aboriginal stockman.

"Hey, Kamulla!" he called.

Kamulla answered in his quiet voice.

"G'day there, Spindles."

"Kamulla, can you tell me something?"

"Do me best," Kamulla smiled back, his white teeth shining against his dark skin. Strange, thought Spindles, that even though his teeth are not really white at all, his smile seems brighter than any white man's.

"Kamulla," Spindles began, "do you know why we have Christmas parties?"

"Nothin' to do with me, lad. If the Boss wants to 'ave a party, that's 'is business, I reckon."

"But you must have some idea!"

"I think it's somethin' to do with religion, Spindles. When I was at the Mission school, they told us about Jesus Christ—isn't Christmas somethin' about his birth or death or somethin'?"

This sounded vaguely familiar to Spindles and he remembered that his Correspondence School lessons had mentioned it, too. But his mum had told him to skip over those bits. "You don't need to know that stuff to get an education," she had said.

"Kamulla, can you tell me more about . . ."

But Kamulla had quietly disappeared, the extent of his religious knowledge having been thoroughly covered in his one short statement.

Spindles couldn't understand it.

He could ask Butch about shearing, and he would talk to him for hours. Captain never seemed in a hurry to get rid of him at other times. Even Lonely would sit with him as long as he liked, just to be with him, or even to talk about the stillness and loneliness of the bush in the clear summer nights, or the sound of animals in the distance, or the brilliant canopy of the outback sky.

But today, they all seemed to have something more important to do.

Spindles was puzzled.

After lunch, he saddled his pony and rode out towards Dusty Range, a line of low, sharp hills that stretched like a lazy dinosaur across the plain about five kilometres from the station. Here there were a couple of rock pools, and winding rows of enormous, strong redgum trees following the creek beds that stumbled down from the untidy hills. The creeks were usually dry, but there was wild life in the area, and you could always find a shady spot where there was a bit of breeze.

He had not been there long, when he saw his friend Roo.

"Hello Spindles," she greeted him.

"G'day, Roo," he answered.

They half-dozed there for a while—for most animals do not find it necessary to talk all the time as humans do. Then Spindles had an inspiration. Perhaps Roo would be able to tell him something about Christmas!

"Roo! Can you tell me why people have Christmas parties?"

"Well, child, I don't know that I can. But I can tell you something about Christmas."

"You can! Go on then!"

"Well," Roo began, "I have a little joey in my pouch, and he reminds me of the time when the baby Jesus was born to the Virgin Mary."

"I've heard something about that. But who was Jesus?"

"Who was Jesus? Don't you know?" (Roo seemed very surprised, and Spindles thought he had asked a stupid question.)

She went on, "Jesus was the Son of God. But he started life just like anyone else—like

you, for example. Except that his real Father was not a man, but God."

"What do you mean?"

"Well, when his mother had a baby in her womb, she was not married. But she was happy, because an angel had told her that her baby was started by God."

Spindles partly understood this. Although his parents had not told him anything about Jesus, they had told him about the way babies are born—in fact, he was very knowledgeable on the subject, and rather proud of it. But here was something new. A baby whose Father was God! Just then, a flock of galahs came screeching through the sky, and settled on a great redgum tree nearby—it was as if the whole tree suddenly burst into flower, with beautiful pink, grey and white petals. The birds were chattering so much that it's a wonder they even noticed the boy and the kangaroo.

But one or two of them did and flew down to join them.

"G'day, Spindles," cried one, whose eyes were bright and whose feathers were brilliantly coloured. The pink seemed on fire, the white was without blemish and the grey as smooth as silk.

"G'day, Gleam," said Spindles.

"Hello, Gleam," said Roo. She was very polite even though she didn't really like all the noise.

"What are you talking about?" Gleam asked.

"Christmas—" began Spindles. But he got no further. Immediately the galah was chattering away.

"Christmas! Of course. It's Christmas Day tomorrow. Did I ever tell you what I like most about Christmas?"

He did not wait for an answer, but went right on talking.

"You know how we galahs fill the sky with our wheeling and turning and diving and floating. And you know the sun reflects from our magnificent colours. And we fill the sky with movement. Well, when I'm flying there I think of the angels who filled the sky on the night Jesus was born! 'Glory to God in the Highest,' they sang. Well, now I must admit their voices probably sounded a bit better than ours—although, mind you, our voices are not that bad, and we can imitate other people pretty well, although angels are a bit above our level—now as I was saying before you sidetracked me—"

Spindles didn't even have time to object at this injustice, for Gleam went right on.

"When we galahs fill the sky, I can't help remembering the angels who filled the sky with God's glory, for the Son of God was born to bring peace and good will to man!"

And the thought of this made Gleam so excited that he screeched out, as only a galah can, and flew up into the sky.

Immediately the petals all seemed to float from the tree, caught up into the clear, deep blue above, while hundreds of galah voices ranged the sky with a united song of "Glory to God in the Highest!"

And as he watched them, Spindles thought that the sound of angels could not have been more beautiful. And the brilliance of angels in the sky could not have excelled the glowing pinks and greys against the measureless vault of heaven!

Meanwhile, Gawk, the emu, had wandered along the creek bed. Spindles was glad to see him, for emus are delightfully friendly creatures, with a keen sense of fun.

"What's all the noise about, Spins?" he wanted to know.

"Well, the galahs have just been telling me about Christmas."

"Oh. Well, that is something to make a noise about indeed."

"What do you mean?"

"Well, Christmas is a happy time of the year for me. For although I often think about Jesus, at Christmas in particular, I remember him. Especially the way some people hated him."

"That's a funny thing to remember," thought Spindles. But he thought it aloud, and Gawk heard him.

"Not at all," he commented. "Especially if you are an emu."

"How come?"

"Well, people often laugh at emus. 'Look at the funny bird,' they say. They try and lure us into doing stupid tricks. Do you know I once saw some people lying on their backs kicking their feet in the air to attract a flock of emus over to them to see what was going on! And they call *us* funny!"

"What about—er—Jesus?"

"Well, people used to mock him, too. When he was just a baby, King Herod made out he wanted to worship him, but he really wanted to kill him. Then when he was grown up, people sneered at him because he was 'just a carpenter.' And then they brought false charges against him and finally condemned him to death. But that wasn't all—they put a crown of thorns on his head and a kingly robe on him. And they tried to get him to do magic tricks. They made fun of him."

"But why, Gawk? Why did they do all that?"

"Because he was good, and upright, and generous—and especially because he told the truth! People don't like to be told the truth, you know."

Spindles remembered how the people at home had tried to get away from him so quickly before. Didn't they like the truth either?

"Talking of sending Jesus to his death, I would like to say something about that." The voice was deep, strong and kind. It made Spindles feel very safe. He and Gawk and Roo all turned around to face the giant Redgum tree that stood behind them.

It was the tree who was talking! They all listened respectfully, in silence. Redgum did not speak often, and when he did, he did not like to be hurried or interrupted. After a few moments, the great tree went on.

"When Jesus was born, he was laid in a wooden feed box, because they had no cot. When he grew up, he became a carpenter, using wood to make things. When he preached, he sometimes preached from a wooden boat. It was in a wooden boat that he calmed the storm on Galilee. And it was on a cross of wood that he was crucified.

"I am proud that Jesus used wood during his life. But I am hurt that they used wood to bring him to his death. The nails that they drove into his hands brought pain to the wooden cross as well.

"Yet I know that it was only because he died on a cross that he was able to save

people from their sins. So whenever I think of Christmas, I do not only think of the cradle—I think of the cross."

Then the big tree was silent. And only his strong, firm arms reaching up to the sky seemed to be saying, "I worship you, my God," while the leaves seemed to whisper, "Thank you, Jesus."

No one dared speak for a while. Finally, in a low voice, Spindles asked, "Why did they kill him if he was the Son of God?"

"Do you remember how your dad punishes you when you are naughty?" asked Roo.

"Yes, indeed." And Spindles had his hands over his buttocks as he answered.

"Well," suggested Gawk, "what if one day one of the station hands stood in your place and took the spanking for you?"

"That'd be beaut," agreed Spindles.

"Well, that's what Jesus did!" Roo was talking again now. "All people are sinners, and have disobeyed God, but God let Jesus take the punishment instead! So if we accept this, we can be forgiven and live forever!"

"That's good news, isn't it?" suggested Gawk.

"It sure is," agreed Spindles.

The sun was beginning to set, and Spindles knew that it was time to go home. So he mounted his pony and headed slowly on his way.

That night the party went ahead in full swing. Friends and stockmen had come from neighbouring stations, and all seemed to be having a happy time. There was eating and drinking, dancing and joking, laughing and shouting. Gifts were exchanged and news shared.

It wasn't much fun for a boy, however, so Spindles—after he had eaten all he could, of course—wandered out on the verandah.

He sat down in the still evening, very thoughtful. The sky above was a deep black, with a thousand sparkling stars scattered over it. In the distance, the occasional sound of a restless bird could be heard. A few minutes later (or was it longer?) he saw someone walking down the track towards the house. He thought at first it was a late guest, but it was no one he knew.

The man walked to the window and looked in. A couple of people seemed to see him, but then turned aside and tried to ignore him. The man moved to the door, and tried to go in. But some men were standing around the door, and barred his way. When he gently attempted to ease past them, they turned their backs and made no attempt to move. When he was finally able to reach the inside of the room where the party was being held, hardly anyone looked at him, and those who did were obviously embarrassed by his presence and tried to act as though they hadn't seem him at all.

Finally, he turned away, and left the house. Some people breathed obvious sighs of relief.

The man wandered slowly back down the track.

With a shock, Spindles realised that he was wearing a purple robe and a crown of thorns.

He ran after him, but he was gone.

And slowly Spindles thought he heard the deep voice of the old Redgum saying slowly,

He was in the world
and the world was made through him,
and the world knew him not.
He came to his own home,
and his own people received him not.
But to all who received him,
who believed in his name,
He gave power to become the children of God.
      (John 1:10-12)

2

Spindles Rides a Race

At a quarter past six on Christmas morning, Spindles was wide awake. He had actually been awake since about five o'clock. He was thinking, of course, about the gifts that he hoped to receive. And he was so excited, that he just couldn't go back to sleep.

But he was also thinking about the Christmas party that his parents had held the night before.

How could people keep Christmas without thinking about Jesus Christ?

Why wouldn't they let Jesus into the party?

Weren't they grateful for his birth in a manger and his death on a cross?

And why had he really died anyway?

Spindles still didn't fully understand.

His mind drifted back again to Christmas gifts. Finally, he just couldn't stay in bed any longer.

So he crept into the lounge room. He wasn't actually going to *open* anything. He just wanted to guess by the shape of the packages what he was going to receive. But there was one gift that needed no guessing at all. For there alongside the Christmas tree was a shiny, new, purple dragster bike! Wow!

Forgetting all about his parents' warnings not to wake them up before eight o'clock, he burst into their bedroom, his unbuttoned pajama coat trailing behind him like a loose sail, and bounced on to their big, double bed.

"Gee, Dad! A new bike! What a beauty—"

He stopped. Dad was slowly sitting up.

"Timothy!"

"Yes, Dad?"

"What time is it?"

"Well, it's—er—it's . . ."

"Well?"

"Sorry, Dad," mumbled Spindles and backed out of the room. He couldn't understand why, if parties were such good fun, people were so grumpy the next morning. Especially Christmas morning. Oh well, he'd have to find something else to do until everyone was up.

So he scampered into his room, threw off his pajamas, grabbed the same shorts and shirt he had worn the day before (Mum wouldn't notice—anyway, they looked clean enough to him), tiptoed back into the lounge, and gazed at his new gift. He stroked it lovingly, and wheeled it round the room. He was supposed not to touch anything until his parents got up. But they wouldn't be up for ages. Gently, he eased the bike through the doorway, down the passage and out the back door.

And then he was on it and riding around the yard. A couple of squawking chickens fled as he charged them, furiously ringing the bell. Captain roared at him as he rode past the kitchen door just as he was opening it. His pony looked at him wistfully over the fence—as if envious of his new machine.

"Hey, Spindles! You want something to eat?" Captain's voice brought Spindles skidding to the kitchen door for breakfast.

"What do you think of my new bike?" he managed to ask between mouthfuls.

"Me? I'll stick to 'orses," answered the cook. But then, seeing Spindles look a bit disappointed at his lack of enthusiasm, he hastily added, "But for you, it's real beaut. Best one I've ever seen."

It was, in fact, the only dragster the cook had ever seen. But as Spindles didn't know that, he was very impressed.

After breakfast, Spindles decided he would show off his new possession. Mum and Dad were still in bed, so he looked for someone else.

But it seemed as though everyone was still asleep. Except Lonely.

"It's all right, Spins," he said slowly, looking at the bike. And from Lonely, that was really something, for he was a man of few words.

So Spindles decided to ride out to Dusty Range. The morning sun was not yet strong enough to have burned the blue from the hills, and they still seemed more purple than brown. He pedalled off down the track. With his pony, he always had to open the gate. Now he could ride straight across the grid. It was bumpy, but quick.

After about twenty minutes he reached the creek bed and pulled up under the shade of some redgums.

The animals, of course, had seen him coming and soon joined him there. Gawk was a bit suspicious of the bike. He had seen motor vehicles and he knew Lonely's motorbike. But they at least made a noise. This bicycle was too silent and mysterious by far. Roo was rather scornful of all mechanical transport and hardly seemed interested at all. Tank, the goanna, opened one eye, blinked, and then closed it again.

"What is it?" asked Gawk.

"A bike, of course!" Spindles answered.

"A bike. Of course. I should have known. Now what, may I ask, do you do with a bike?"

"A bike? Ride it, of course! Can't you see?"

And noting Gawk's still puzzled expression, Spindles went on to explain.

"You sit on the seat, like this—"

"Me? Sit on that? Not likely."

And when he thought of it, the idea of an emu riding a bike did seem somewhat strange. In fact, it wasn't just strange, it was hilarious! He burst out laughing. He laughed till tears slid from his eyes. He laughed till he had to lean on the bike for support.

Gawk, meanwhile, who had a keen sense of humor himself, disdained to laugh, and put on his most dignified look. The sight of an emu trying to look dignified amused Spindles even more.

When he had regained control of himself, Spindles again tried to explain.

"I sit on the seat like this," he began, with the emphasis on the "I." "Then I place my feet on these pedals, and push them. This turns the chain, which drives the rear wheel, and then the bike moves—like this."

And he was off, down the creek bed, around a large rock, and back again into the shade of the trees.

Gawk eyed him carefully, while Roo, who had been pretending to take no notice at all,

watched him out of the corner of her eye. And the huge Redgum stood silently surveying the whole scene, saying nothing, but missing nothing either.

"Tell you what," shouted Spindles. "I reckon I can go faster than you."

Now if there's one thing emus are proud of, it's their speed. "That's why we don't have wings," Gawk often said. "We can run so fast, we don't need 'em." So a challenge to race is, for an emu, almost irresistible.

"Faster than me? On that thing? Never!"

"All right, then," answered Spindles. "Let's see!"

So they worked out a plan for a race. They were to start at the Redgum, follow the creek bed to the track—a distance of about twenty metres—then race in the open along the track to the fence—nearly a kilometre away—and back again. The first one to Redgum would be the winner. Roo was starter.

"When I thump my tail on the ground, start," she instructed them.

So Gawk scratched a line on the ground with his big toe, and he and Spindles lined up ready to race.

"Ready. Set. Thump!"

And away they went.

Gawk was away first. Little clouds of dust hung over the spots where his six long toes had been. There were scratch marks on the ground. And a couple of creek-stones were still rolling away. He himself was metres down the creek. His long neck was held upright, his small wings were pressed close to his sides and his legs swung backwards and forwards like scissor blades.

Spindles was in trouble. A creek bed is not the best place for riding a bike—especially a new one. The pebbles were small and smooth and the wheels of the bike sank into them. Every now and then there were large rocks to be avoided. When he made it to the track, Gawk seemed to be halfway to the fence already, but Spindles was now racing at top speed. The chrome shone in the sun, and the purple glowed like the feathers of a parrot flashing among the trees. He put his head down and forced his legs to move faster. He felt his thigh muscles straining and his lungs groping for breath. His usually untidy hair was blown out of his eyes by the breeze he himself was producing. And his long spindly legs seemed part of the machine itself.

Gawk reached the fence and was so confident that he stopped and waited for Spindles. His bulging eyes shone with confidence and mischief as he called out things like, "Come on slowcoach!" Or, "That thing would go better if it had legs!" Or, "Why don't you put some energy into it, Spins?"

Spindles was too short of breath to answer. He slammed on the brakes, spun the bike around, showering red dust all over Gawk, and immediately set off to race back towards the creek. Gawk didn't waste any more time. His long legs thrust out before him, he strode after Spindles, his body swaying as he ran, so that he seemed to be going slower than he really was.

A flock of galahs drifted across the sky, and swept down to see what was happening. Below them they could see Gawk striding along in the sunshine, his large steps eating into the track. Just in front of him was Spindles, like a great purple and white beetle shimmering his way along. If you didn't know better, you would have thought that the beetle was trying to escape from the bird.

The galahs plunged down from the blue into the line of trees that marked the creek bed, waiting for the two racers to reach the shade.

The sun was hotter now, and sweat was gathering on Spindles' forehead. Even Gawk, who was used to the heat, was looking forward to reaching the trees, where the galahs sat chattering and squawking.

They reached the creek together.

Spindles, remembering how the emu had got away from him in the creek bed before, put all his effort into the last twenty metres. He had to agree that legs were better than wheels in rough country!

Ten metres. Still level. He'd make it yet.

Five metres from the end was a clump of boulders, left there years before by some freak flood that had rolled them playfully down from the hills, only to abandon them like toys on the bedroom floor. There was just room for both of them to pass between the boulders together. But as they did, the left pedal on Spindles' dragster caught a jutting edge on one of the rough rocks. His right foot was jarred from the other pedal. The handle bars slewed round.

The front wheel rammed into rock. The bike stopped suddenly, but Spindles did not! He tumbled over the top of the bike, and fell heavily.

As he did, there was a smart crack, like the snapping of a stick. But it was not a stick. It was Spindles' right arm. It was broken!

The galahs rose up in fright, squawking and screeching. Gleam, Spindles' old friend, plunged down to his side. Roo was there too, with a single hop. And Gawk, who had crossed the line and thought the galahs were cheering him for winning, was only a second behind Roo as soon as he realised what had happened.

Spindles lay groaning. His face was as white as a summer cloud and he was fighting for breath.

His beautiful new bike lay dusty and scratched, the front wheel bent out of shape, and the fork angled backwards instead of forwards.

Roo bent down, and with her short, but strong forearms, dragged him gently back into the shade of the Redgum tree. The other trees seemed to lean forward in an effort to increase the shade, and the breeze wafted through the leaves so that they whispered, "Don't worry, Spindles, don't worry, Spindles . . . ." And even the galahs were quiet, while Gleam murmured, "We'll help you, Spins. Don't you get upset. We'll look after you."

But no one really knew what to do. Spindles would not be able to walk five kilometres through the heat. It was no good any of the animals trying to talk to the men at the station. If an emu or a kangaroo tried to attract their attention they would be quite ignored—or even worse, possibly shot at by Butch, who saw emus and roos as problems, not friends.

And as for galahs—who ever took them seriously?

But Redgum knew what to do.

"Gawk," he said. At the sound of his strong, deep voice, everyone was silent.

"You have powerful legs. Why don't you carry Spindles back to the homestead and leave him where someone will find him? You can do it—and only you can do it. There is no one else."

The big tree was once again silent.

But everyone knew that there was nothing more to say. Only Gawk could help Spindles now. And if he didn't, no one else could.

"Do you think you can hang on to me, if Roo lifts you on to my back?" Gawk asked Spindles.

"I don't know," Spindles answered, in too much pain to be able to think clearly.

"Well, will you try?"

Spindles bit his lip and nodded.

So Roo took him in her arms and lifted him.

Spindles cried out with the pain, but he knew it had to be done, so he gritted his teeth, and tried to be quiet.

"Lift your leg, Spins."

He managed to get his right leg up and over Gawk's back. He wound his left arm around the great bird's neck. His right arm rested down his side—where it still hurt dreadfully, but at least the feathers were soft.

And so they set off.

Gawk picked his way carefully along the stony creek bed. He kept to the soft patches where small creek-stones, almost like sand, lay smoothed by a thousand years of wind and

rain. Grey, brown, red, blue, green—they lay in all colours, a carpet for the emu's feet. He reached the track, and took a deep breath. He was a sturdy bird, but he had just raced over a kilometre, and he now had five kilometres to walk in the hot sun—and he had to walk slowly and carefully, ever mindful of the burden he carried on his back.

The sun rose higher. Spindles grew hotter and more feverish. His grip seemed to loosen.

"Hang on, mate!" Gawk urged him. "Soon be there!"

Spindles gripped his neck again, and they continued on.

One kilometre.

Two kilometres.

Three kilometres.

Four kilometres.

And the sun rose still higher in the sky.

Spindles seemed to be losing consciousness.

Gawk began to feel weak, but he had to continue. He had to hurry before the lad collapsed altogether.

"Don't let go, Spins!"

"I won't." But even as he spoke, Spindles' grip seemed to loosen.

"There's the gate, now. Only a few more metres."

"Uh? All right, Gawk . . . I'll try . . . ."

Spindles was nearly finished. If Gawk didn't put him down, he would fall off.

Gawk was so intent on caring for Spindles and looking ahead to the homestead that, for a few paces, he forgot to watch the ground closely. And so he did something that no emu ever did.

Lying on the hot ground of the track was the sheening silver-and-brown-striped body of a tiger snake. The December heat had made it sleepy and it hadn't heard the emu coming. The first either of them knew was that Gawk had trodden on the snake.

His immediate reaction was to jump, lash out with his long claws, strike, kill. But with an injured boy on his back he could do none of those things.

So he lifted his foot slowly. He let the snake glide away. But he knew that nothing mattered any more. For fang marks showed on his leg where the snake had bitten him. Gawk's life was nearly over.

Spindles knew little of what had happened.

In his dazed condition, he was aware only of a short stop, and then the swaying motion of Gawk's loping walk again. The emu reached the gate, stepped over the grid, and slowly wandered into the homestead.

Captain saw him first.

"Hey! Will you look at that!" he said to no one in particular. "An emu coming right into the house yard! Strike me pink, they're getting bolder every day. What in the world does—"

Captain broke off. Suddenly he saw Spindles. Forgetting the strangeness of the situation, he raced up to the bird.

Gawk squatted down, and Spindles slid to the ground. The cook saw the queer shape of the boy's arm.

"Stone the crows, Spins," he said. "What have you done to yourself?" And taking no notice of Gawk at all, he stooped, lifted Spindles gently and carried him towards the house shouting, "Hey boss! Lonely! Butch! Someone! Spindles has busted 'is arm. Quick! Boss! Come 'ere, quick."

Doors slammed. People converged on the spot from all directions. Somebody ran to call the Flying Doctor. Somebody else got a drink. Others talked, waved their arms, shouted advice, and generally got in the way.

And Gawk turned, and wandered slowly towards the gate.

He was dimly aware of voices in the background.

"An emu brought him in? Don't be daft!"

"Where is it then?"

"It was just 'ere a minute ago."

"Next thing you'll be seein' pink elephants too."

"What do you mean, he came in riding an emu?"

"There it is!"

This last voice was Captain's. He was pointing to Gawk, who had reached the grid, but was having difficulty crossing it. He managed to scrape his way across, but he could go no further. He dropped down just beyond it, his long neck sagging, and his eyes drooping. Gone was the mischief and light of those big eyes. Gone was the impertinent pride of former days.

By the time the men reached him, he was dead.

A week later, Spindles was allowed to get around by himself again. His arm was in plaster, in a sling, and his damaged cycle was waiting in the blacksmith's shop for repairs. The station hand who did this sort of work was away for a month.

But it didn't matter. Spindles couldn't ride it at the moment anyway. Nor did he want to, particularly. So he was back on his old faithful pony. The horse was so quiet that it was safe to ride him, even with one arm in a sling. They headed out to the creek bed again.

"Never should have wanted a bike in the first place," Spindles said to the pony. "Would have been a lot safer on you."

But the pony gave no answer.

"Now I've lost one of my best friends."

Still no answer.

But the look in his pony's eyes said, "I could have told you all that."

When they reached the shade of the trees, the pony was turned loose to graze, and Spindles sat in his favourite spot under Redgum.

"Why didn't Gawk kill the snake?" he demanded of no one in particular. "He could have done it easily."

He couldn't ask these questions at home, for although they knew that an emu had been there when Spindles returned and that the bird had died, no one really knew why.

The general opinion was that Spindles had walked back from the creek, and that he had imagined the whole story about the race with Gawk. The cook's idea that the emu had carried Spindles was clearly impossible. He must have been seeing things.

So Spindles had to talk to someone who would believe him.

"Why?" he demanded again. "It was my stupid idea to have the race in the first place. I know that. But why did Gawk have to die just because of that! Why did he do it?"

Redgum let him talk for a while. It was no good saying anything until Spindles was ready to listen. Finally, the boy was at last quiet.

"Spindles."

It was the voice of Redgum.

"Yes, Redgum?"

"Do you remember how you once asked all your friends about Christmas?"

"Yes."

"And do you remember how Gawk and Roo tried to explain to you why Jesus Christ came into the world?"

"Yes."

"Well, on Christmas Day, Gawk showed you the meaning of Christmas in a way far better than he could ever have told you."

"What do you mean, Redgum?"

"Do you have a Bible at home, Spindles?"

"Somewhere."

"When you get home, will you look up two verses from the Bible? I think you will find your answers."

"All right, Redgum. I'll try. What are the verses?"

Later that day, Spindles found a Bible in the bottom corner of the family bookcase—the darkest corner of the room. He lugged it with his left hand into his bedroom, sprawled out on the bed, and looked up the passages that Redgum had given him. It wasn't easy, for he could only use one hand, and he didn't know his way around the Bible anyway. But he finally found the first one.

And this is what he read:

Greater love has no man than this,
That a man lay down his life for his friends.
(John 15:13)

"So that's why Gawk did it," thought
Spindles. "Because he loved me."
And he thought about that for a long time.
Then he began to search for the other
passage that Redgum had given him. He turned
a lot of pages before he finally located it. What
he read was this:

While we were yet helpless,
At the right time,
Jesus died for the ungodly.
Why, one will hardly die for a righteous man—
Though perhaps for a good man one will even
dare to die.
But God shows his love for us
In that while we were yet sinners
Christ died for us.
(Romans 5:5-8)

And now Spindles began to understand a
little more.
"Thank you, Gawk," he whispered. "And
Jesus—thank you, too."

3

Spindles and the Lost Joey

"Beauty," said Spindles. "No school today."

Not that Spindles really went to school.

He did his lessons by correspondence, at home. But his mother was as strict as any school teacher. Lessons started and finished on time. And while they were on, Spindles had to work. He even had homework as well!

"How can you give me homework when all my school work is homework?" he had once asked his mother.

This seemed a perfectly reasonable question to him. But his mother told him not to be cheeky.

However, today was Saturday. And that meant no lessons. So he lay in bed wondering what he would do. He knew that there was really only one thing he could do. He would go out to the Dusty Range again—where he always went. But he liked to think of other possibilities, even though he would probably never follow them through.

He was there by nine o'clock. There were a few galahs fluttering about among the trees. A flock of white cockatoos chattered their way across the sky, thrown into the air like a packet of white confetti. A sleepy lizard lay basking in a patch of sunshine between the shade of two of the creek trees, as if it had been there undisturbed for centuries. A couple of his father's sheep were browsing, their heads lowered, for the day was already hot. And Redgum stood silent and majestic, guardian of the Range.

Spindles plucked a twig with a few leaves on it from a sapling, sat under Redgum's huge trunk, and flicked lazily at the little black bush flies that silently darted around his eyes and ears.

He missed Gawk.

The place didn't seem the same without him.

Oh, there were other emus, of course. Hippie, for instance, was good fun. He liked to laugh and play, make puns and perform practical jokes. But he wasn't as old as Gawk had been and sometimes you needed older friends to give you advice and tell you when to stop. Still, Hippie was a pretty good emu.

But Spindles still missed Gawk.

I wonder if Roo misses Gawk as much as I do? thought Spindles. And then he realised that he hadn't seen Roo yet. She would probably turn up before the morning was out.

Spindles had something he wanted to ask Roo. For he was still puzzled about the story of Jesus. The way Gawk had given his life to get Spindles home safely had meant a lot to him. But he still didn't really see why Jesus had to die to save people. And just what exactly was it that people needed saving from? If God loved people, why didn't he just accept them anyway?

These were big questions for a boy, and he soon grew tired of trying to answer them. When Roo came, she would help him.

There was a rustling noise in the prickly spinifex grass just up the hill. And bursting through the grass came Roo.

How can she go through that stuff without being scratched? thought Spindles. *It sticks into me like needles.*

But Roo pushed through the sharp, long-pointed clumps of spinifex as though they were the softest feathers. She hopped quickly down to where Spindles was in the creek bed, but without her usual sprightliness.

Spindles could see that something was wrong.

"Roo! What's the matter?"

"Spindles! Can you help me? I've lost Joey!"

"Joey? Lost! How? What do you mean? You can't have lost him! Not Joey."

"I've been looking all night, but I can't find him anywhere. Oh, child, what will I do?"

Roo's voice always sounded so calm and reassuring that Spindles was upset to hear the anguish in her speech now. He knew that this was a serious problem.

"Where did you lose him? How did it happen?"

"At the Opal Rock Pool, yesterday morning. I was attacked by a dingo. Joey and I were separated and—"

"A dingo!" exclaimed Spindles.

"Yes, a dingo," answered Roo. "And then when—"

Roo was interrupted, not by Spindles, but by Redgum.

"Roo, you are exhausted. Sit down here in the shade for a while, and when you feel refreshed, tell us slowly everything that happened and we will see what we can do to help."

Spindles was always amazed at the way Redgum's voice seemed to take the tension out of everything. Whenever there was a problem or a crisis, he seemed to know just what to say and what to do. And it always seemed that everything would be all right, when he spoke.

Roo did as she was told. Redgum was not the sort of person you could argue with. She licked her wrists and smoothed down her fur. She squatted down, picked some grass with her front paws and raised it to her mouth.

After a while she said, "I'm ready to tell you now."

There was no answer, so she began.

"Well, yesterday morning, I went up to the Opal Rock Pool to drink. It was a beautiful, calm morning, you remember, with a freshness in the air that made everything sing. As usual, I checked to see that there was no danger. I sensed nothing out of the ordinary. So I drank and then hopped away under a few scrub trees to rest. Little Joey hopped out of the pouch and we both fed for a while. He's four months old now, you know, and he's becoming quite independent.

"The pool was like a mirror: the grey-green of the trees and the thick blue of the sky were perfectly reflected. There wasn't a murmur of breeze. You could hear birds from three kilometres away over the Range. I even picked out the sound of something banging at the homestead. It clacked across the morning air as clear as you like. So I relaxed. If there had been

anything moving through the bush I would have heard it. The only near sounds were the slight movements of a few of the other kangaroos—and I ought to know them by now.

"So I began to doze. Every now and then, I opened one eye to see how Joey was getting on. As I did this the last time, I thought I saw a faint movement in the shade of the big boulders at the northern end of the pool. I was just about to close my eyes, when I saw this movement again. There was no mistake this time. So I watched closely.

"There, in the shade of the rocks was a dingo! He must have been there since dark, patiently waiting. And I could see that he was edging himself into a position where he could spring down on us.

"I called Joey quietly to me. He came and hopped into the pouch. Slowly I moved towards the top of the hill, so that I could slip over to the other side and escape."

In his mind's eye, Spindles could clearly see Roo carefully putting her front paws on the ground and swinging her hind legs forward; then resting on her hind legs while she reached forward with her front paws again; then again swinging the hind legs forward. And he could see Joey peeking out over the top of the pouch, keeping his eye on the dingo.

But Roo was continuing.

"We were approaching the hill top, when the dingo sprang up and threw himself towards us. I could see his fierce white teeth, his yellow-brown fur, his bushy tail, his flashing eyes. Without a moment's hesitation, I fled at top speed—up, over the hill and down the other side."

And again, in his imagination, Spindles could see what happened. He could picture Roo taking giant leaps through the low scrub. She cleared boulders and fallen branches with no effort. Spinifex grass was crushed beneath her feet. Pebbles rolled away in the dust after the great thrust of her hind legs. Her front paws were no longer being used, except for balance. Her back legs, like two giant springs, propelled her metres at a time. And behind her raced the dingo. He ran close to the ground under the branches that Roo jumped; around the rocks that she cleared; and over the dry and ragged undergrowth that she crushed underfoot. His red tongue lolled from his mouth and his powerful jaws seemed ready to crush the kangaroo. He ran so smoothly, he could keep going all day.

"For a while, I kept well ahead," Roo continued. "But Joey is getting bigger now. And with him in my pouch I could neither run nor jump at top speed. So I had to do something or we would have both been lost. I came to a part of the creek bed between the hills where there were a few large rocks and where thousands of small stones lay over a wide clear area. I made sure that the dingo could see me, and while I was running, I picked Joey out of my pouch and threw him to one side—"

"What in the world did you do that for?" demanded Spindles. "The dingo would have caught him easily. He isn't old enough to escape from—"

"Let me finish," said Roo. "You see, Spindles, I had a plan. When I threw Joey out, the dingo paused a little. He didn't know whether to chase me or Joey. I guess he thought I would make a better meal, but then Joey would be easier to catch. Joey meanwhile, was off up the other side of the gorge, and had a good start. Even so, the dingo looked as though he was going to follow him. Then I stumbled."

"You stumbled! Now you were in trouble too!"

"No, I did it deliberately. I made it seem as though I had overbalanced. I kicked with my hind legs and threw up a lot of small stones. I struggled harder, but seemed as though I couldn't get up.

"When the dingo saw this, he forgot about Joey and headed for me. As soon as the dingo started running towards me, I thrust down hard and sprang into the air. With two leaps, I was out of the creek bed and up the hill—the way we had come, and away from Joey."

"I get it!" interrupted Spindles. "You wanted to give Joey plenty of time to get away."

"Yes, and I did, too. Joey was too far from the dingo by this time. He was safe. But I wasn't. And it became a desperate struggle for me. I don't know how long I raced through the Range. No matter what tricks I tried, or how fast I moved, that yellow-brown dog was close behind me. I thought I would never escape.

"But then a miracle happened. From the top of one of the hills, I saw Lonely riding his motorbike beside a fence. So I headed in that direction immediately. It was still touch and go. Going downhill is harder sometimes than going up. I landed in some loose scree, and the whole lot began to slither down, taking me with it. I nearly lost my footing altogether. This gave the dingo time to get within a couple of metres, but I managed to keep just in front of him.

"Finally we reached the plain. I don't think the dingo expected me to go that way. He thought I would stick to the hills. But I knew that Lonely and his dog would rather attack the dingo than me so I ran straight towards them.

"Sleepy saw us first. He sprang off the back of the bike and charged the dingo. Sleepy doesn't look very lively, but when it comes to a fight, he's a new animal. He flew at the dingo as if it was a cat. When the dingo met Sleepy and saw Lonely behind him on his motor bicycle, carrying a rifle, he realised that he was beaten. He turned around and ran for the bush. Sleepy chased him, but eventually let him go.

"Now I had to find Joey. And I've looked everywhere but I can't find him."

"Didn't he keep the Law?" The question was Redgum's.

"No. He didn't. And I can't understand why."

"Law? What Law?" asked Spindles.

"There must be a reason for it," said Redgum.

"There must be," agreed Roo. "But what can it be? Where can he be? What's happened to him?"

"What Law are you talking about?" demanded Spindles again. "What's that got to do with it?"

"It is the Law of the Bush," explained Roo. "It simply says (in this case) that if animals are separated, they must go back to the place where they first parted and wait there. The place where you separate is the only safe place to meet again."

"Oh . . . Well, didn't Joey do that? Isn't he waiting for you in the gorge?"

"No, child, he's not. And that's why I'm so upset. Something must have happened to him.

"I'll help you look for him!" exclaimed Spindles. And he was about to rush off, when the great tree spoke again:

"Wait, son. Far better for us to organise some kind of search than all go off helter-skelter. We'll need Hippie and Gleam as well. And we must organise a plan of action."

So it was decided. The leaves of the trees passed the word along to the birds and they in turn passed the message further. And it was not long before Hippie and Gleam and their friends had arrived.

Gleam was to organise his fellow galahs in an overhead search. Hippie and the emus were to search the hills. Spindles was to search the plain between the creek and the fence—the scene of his race with Gawk on Christmas Day. Tank was to look wherever he could—especially among the rocks. Whoever found anything was to report immediately to Redgum where there were three galahs waiting to spread the news.

The rest of the galahs took off with a flurry of feathers and noise. They burst into the air like pink and white flares from an exploding firework. And soon they spread out, chattering and gossiping, flying from the southern end of the Dusty Range to the northern end, and back again. And then from east to west. And then along the gorges and creek beds. They wove a colored pattern through the blue sky as if it were an eiderdown.

But they found nothing.

Hippie and a few of his friends set off at their slow gait along the creek bed. As the gorge became more steep and narrow, they had to move more slowly, finally struggling over the rough rocks, and past the sheer faces of red cliffs until they clambered to the top. Then they followed a new gorge down the other side, examining every hole, every small cave or indent in the rock, and every clump of spinifex or tea tree.

But they found nothing.

Tank explored grey rocks and fallen logs. He slithered into crevices and holes; he explored shadows and dark places; he even climbed trees.

But he found nothing.

Spindles mounted his pony, and moved systematically across the flat open plain between the hills and the creek and the fence. It was a kind of triangle, with the fence as the base. Beyond the fence was open space—flat and everlasting.

All day, Spindles searched, until the sun began to sink low in the sky. He knew that he would have to turn for home very soon, or someone would soon be organising a search for him!

But he found nothing.

He didn't know where else to look, so he decided to go back to Redgum and then home. He rode along the fence towards the foot hills intending to ride back along the base of the Range rather than following the track. Perhaps Joey was hidden somewhere there.

He had gone almost as far as he could along the fence, and was about to turn, when he noticed that the wires of the fence near him were moving, as if someone further up was standing on them. So, curious, he dismounted, and walked a little way into the hills, to see if there was someone or something there.

He had climbed about twenty metres when he saw the wires move again. And there in front of him was Joey!

The poor little creature was tangled in the wires of the fence.

When his mother had flung him from the pouch, he had hit the ground hard, tumbling over once or twice. But he needed no one to tell him what to do. Even while he was still spinning, his feet were groping for a firm grip. Within seconds he was sprinting up the hill, plunging through spinifex and mimosa, banging against rocks, and catching himself on the twigs of low hanging branches. He had but one aim—to get as far from danger as possible.

Soon he was over the hill, and although he heard nothing behind him, he plunged down the other side, head extended, and his young, but strong hind legs thrusting him in little leaps over rock and bush. Every nerve was strained, every muscle exerted to reach safety. Soon he had gained the foot of the hill and he sped along the fringe of the plain. He fled so desperately that he completely failed to see the fence looming up in front of him. He ran straight into it. The force of the impact spun him round so hard that he twisted two wires together. And between the twist was his foot—caught fast.

He had been there nearly two days now. He was thirsty, dirty, exhausted, ragged and bleeding. Flies burrowed into the dried blood. Sunlight reddened his weary eyes. His lips were cracked and sore, his throat shrivelled and dry. He was too weak to cry out. His life was almost gone! Only his desperate continuing struggle to be free had moved the wires and attracted Spindles' attention.

Where he lay he was partly covered by scrub, and thus the galahs had missed him. The emus had also overlooked him. Had

Spindles not seen the faint moving of the fence wire, he would have ridden past him too.

Spindles dropped to his knees.

"You poor little chap!" he cried. "It's a wonder you're still alive." And he gently lifted the wires back so that Joey's foot was freed—a task which was not easy, because the wires gripped tightly. It took all Spindles' strength to do it.

Joey's leg was cut through to the bone. He could not possibly walk on it. So Spindles picked him up in his arms and carried him down the hill to where his pony stood waiting. He managed to climb on without dropping the little kangaroo, and although he wanted to ride as fast as he could, he could only go at walking pace, back to Redgum. Before he arrived he shouted out, "I've found him! I've found him! Redgum! Gleam! Hippie! I've found Joey!"

Within moments, a couple of galahs were flying to him, and without even stopping to find out the story, they flew over the Range to tell the rest of the searchers to come back.

In fact, Spindles himself didn't have much time to stop and talk. He had to get home straight away, for it was nearly dark. So he left Joey with Roo and galloped home.

I didn't even have time to say thank you, Roo said to herself a bit later. But she was so busy tending her son, that she soon forgot about that. She would see Spindles again.

It was the following Saturday before Spindles could get to the Range again. He had worried all week about Joey, but he knew that the creatures of the bush have their own ways of healing, and he thought that he would probably be all right. And so he was.

When he arrived, Joey was jumping round again. Mind you, he was favouring one leg, and he didn't try any athletics, but he was obviously recovering.

"What would you have done if you hadn't been stuck in the fence?" Spindles asked him.

"I would have gone back to the gorge where Mother dropped me," Joey replied.

"Why?"

"Because that's the Law of the Bush."

"But how did you know?"

"I don't know. I just know. That's all. It's the Law."

"If you want to meet again, you go back to where you separated?"

"That's right."

And Joey hopped away to a patch of feed that looked especially succulent. Spindles sat under the Redgum in his favourite spot to think. He chewed on a piece of grass.

"I think you have some more answers," said Redgum.

"What do you mean?"

"Well, weren't you wondering last week about why Jesus really came to the earth? Why God didn't handle the situation without sending Jesus?"

"Yes, I was."

"Well, you have learned two things today, haven't you?"

"Two things, Redgum? I've learned one—when two people part, they must go back to their parting-place to meet again."

"Yes. And you've learned something else, too."

Spindles paused to think a bit. Then he continued.

"When someone is lost, someone else has to go and look for him?"

"That's right. There are your answers."

"Redgum, you are very wise. But sometimes you are too wise for me."

"Think about what I have said, Spindles."

"I'll try," said Spindles.

Just then, Roo came up. Spindles got to his feet.

"Spindles, my child. I want to thank you so much for finding Joey."

"I was just lucky, Roo. Anyone could've found him."

"But anyone didn't. You did. Thank you, Spindles."

Spindles didn't know what to say next, so he just stood there scraping the ground with his shoe and hoping somebody would change the subject.

Redgum did.

"Spindles, listen to me. Here are some words from the Bible about Jesus:

Christ Jesus came into the world to save sinners.
(1 Timothy 1:15)

"Spindles, this means, in effect, that Jesus fulfilled the Law of the Bush."

"How?"

"Think, Spindles. Where did people become parted from God?"

"Here, on earth, I suppose."

"Right. So Jesus had to come back here, to the place of parting, to meet us again."

"Oh," said Spindles.

"And here is something from the Bible about the second lesson you have learned. I think you will understand this one:

If a man has a hundred sheep, and one of them is gone astray, does he not leave the ninety and nine, and go in search of the one that went astray?
(Matthew 18:12)

"That one's easy!" agreed Spindles.

And he thought of Joey caught in the fence, and then he imagined that it was he who was caught there. And the person who came to rescue him was Jesus.

4

Spindles and the Flooding Creek

Swish!

Spindles swiped at the little bush fly that was tormenting him; but the fly neatly avoided the streaming gum leaves, and, as soon as Spindles' arm was lowered, continued as before.

Why ever did God make flies? asked Spindles to himself.

Not having any good answer, he took aim again.

This time, the fly was caught unawares and fell crippled to the ground.

"Got him," muttered the boy.

Then once again he settled down to doze under the mottled shadows of the gum trees. He stretched out, wriggled until his back was comfortable, folded his arms under his head, closed his eyes and drifted into daydreams.

Crash! Clatter! Clump!

Spindles sat up with a start.

There was Hippie, parading round him like a newly promoted sergeant, quite ignoring the fact that Spindles was asleep.

"I say, old chap, did I wake you? Awfully sorry."

Spindles had known Hippie for a long time, but he still couldn't quite get used to the emu speaking with an Oxford accent. It didn't seem right, somehow. But then Hippie was an unusual emu.

"What's all the noise about, Hippie?" he asked. "Can't you see when a fellow's asleep?"

"No time for sleeping," Hippie replied. "Today is the first day of the rest of your life, you know. Can't waste it. It's important."

"Today is what?"

"The first day of the rest of your life."

"Very funny."

"No. It's very serious really. Your whole future starts today."

"Well, what if it does? I'm still sleepy."

"You'll sleep your life away. I say, listen. Did you hear the bed creak?"

"What bed?"

"The creek bed, of course."

And Hippie laughed at his own joke, strutting up and down as he did so. "Bed creak . . . creek bed. Get it?" he demanded.

"Oh, Hippie! Cut it out."

"Well, what are you going to do today, Spindles?"

"I'm going to explore the other side of the creek. Then I'll find a nice shady spot. And then I'll go to sleep again."

Hippie thought this was rather strange. Never could he imagine Spindles sleeping during the day when there were things to be done. Spindles was a boy, and boys don't waste daytime hours on such fruitless things as sleeping.

"I say, Spins, are you feeling all right? Not sick? Bit off colour perhaps?"

"No. I'm fine. But I just want to have a sleep."

What Hippie didn't know was that Spindles had been pestering his parents to let him spend a few days in the bush, camping. They had, of course, refused.

"You wouldn't get a wink of sleep all night," his mother had said. "You'd be too scared."

So Spindles was determined to prove that he could sleep in the bush. If he could go home and boast that he had slept all afternoon, they might just change their minds. Of course, they still might not believe him. But he'd work that one out when he came to it.

Spindles climbed to his feet and wandered slowly up the creek bed.

"I say, Spindles, old chap!" called Hippie.

"Yes."

"If you are going to snooze, keep to the high ground, won't you? Never know when a flash flood might come down the creek. Can't have your bath before you get up, you know." And he chuckled again.

At this, Spindles picked up a stone as if to throw it at Hippie. Hippie obligingly made as if to run away. But as he did so he called out again, "It's the Law of the Bush, you know. Keep to high ground."

So Spindles wandered on, a bit sad that Hippie had gone away, but very determined to prove that he was old enough to look after himself.

He knew a grassy spot about a kilometre along the creek, and headed for that. When he arrived, he thought, *This is just the spot.*

So he settled down to snooze again.

He had just become comfortable when he remembered Hippie's words, "Keep to high ground . . . It's the Law."

He remembered that Roo had taught him something similar when Joey had been lost. Joey had broken the Law and had nearly died as a result. But he had saved him. And when the whole world had broken God's law, Jesus Christ had come to save the world. Keeping laws must be important.

And then he realised that he was lying on very low ground. It was shady. It was grassy. It was soft. It was cool. But it was also low.

"Keep to high ground," Hippie had warned him.

But that was only if it was likely to rain. It couldn't rain today. Spindles peered up through the leaves of the trees to the clear, blue sky. Not a cloud anywhere. Deep, endless blue. And high in the sky was the hot summer sun, pouring warmth into the brown earth. It couldn't rain today.

So Spindles stretched out comfortably, closed his eyes, and again tried to sleep. And the harder he tried, the more wide awake he became.

"Blow Hippie," he growled. "I would have been asleep by now if it hadn't been for him."

And then he thought about Hippie, and how good it would be to be racing round the bush with him, or playing with Joey, or climbing rocks, or riding his pony, or even sitting in the kitchen at home with Captain, drinking cordial and eating biscuits, or . . .

And before the shade had moved fifteen centimetres across the ground, Spindles was dead to the world!

Half an hour later, he was still sleeping soundly. So soundly that he did not notice the

clouds sneaking across the sky from the north.
He did not feel the wind rising until it was no
longer a breeze, but a gusty, swirling squall. He
did not notice the dark clouds settling over the
tops of the range. He did not sense the mist
and rain that the hilltops, like huge magnets,
were attracting to themselves. And he did not
know that rivulets of water were beginning to
feel their way around the range looking for
gullies down which they could slide to the plain.

In fact, the first he knew about any of this
was a chilly feeling around the back of his neck.

His hands went through the motions of
pulling the blankets closer round him, but they
couldn't find any blankets. Puzzled, he opened
his eyes. Then he sat up with a shock. There
was water all round him. It was now pouring
down from the ridges, tumbling down the gorge
like a wild goanna, desperate to reach level ground.

He jumped to his feet and tried to escape.
In front of him, on the homestead side of the
creek, was a rock wall about twenty-five
metres high. And between him and the wall
was a swirling stream of brown, muddy water
flowing fast and deep. As he watched, he saw
large rocks beginning to move under the force
of the water. Just in front of him, a stone which
he could never have shifted slowly began to
roll over—so slowly that he could barely see it

move. Then suddenly, with a splash, it was gone, tumbling and bumping its way along. There was no escape in that direction.

Behind him was another stream of water, not so fast and not so deep, but frightening enough for all that. Perhaps he could jump it. He might just make it. He had to do *something*. He was already standing in water up to his ankles, and he could feel the earth being tugged away from beneath his feet.

Now it started to rain. Great heavy drops seemed to be thrown at him from the tree tops. Soon, he was wet through.

He decided to leap across. He took a deep breath and thrust down with all his might. But when he tried to jump, his feet stuck in the mud. One shoe came off. It was the worst jump he had ever done in his life. He landed right in the middle of the water. He overbalanced and fell frontwards. When he hit the water his mouth was open and he was out of breath. He swallowed a great gulp of the muddy water and came up spluttering and coughing. Then he was under again, tumbling over and over, banging his head and his knees and his back and his elbows on stones and rocks as he was carried down by the stream.

The water was not very deep—but it was moving fast, and Spindles just couldn't get his balance. He tried to cry out and only swallowed more water. He tried to grab hold of something and only scraped skin from his fingers. He tried to stand on his feet, but when he put them down there was nothing to put them down on. The whole world seemed to be a confusion of brown water, sticks, stones, gum leaves, rocks, arms, legs, and, not nearly often enough, air.

By this time he was a hundred metres from where he had first fallen. And something flashed into his mind. Hippie had said this was the first day of the rest of his life. The way things were going, it might be the last! And somehow that didn't seem very funny. But just when he thought that his last day really had come, he found that he wasn't moving anymore. He had rammed up against something. It wasn't much—just an old dead gum branch. But it enabled him to get his balance and to stand and breathe again. He stood there in the deep water gulping for breath, trying not to cry, but feeling pain all over his body from the bruises and cuts he had received. He burst into tears.

The water was still pulling at his feet, trying to overbalance him, but he clung to the branch, until he could find something else to do. He had to do something, for the level of the creek

was rising. Above his head he could see bits of debris from a flash flood of three years ago, still caught in the branches of the trees. The water had been very deep then. He had to get out!

But he was still surrounded by water.

Through the trees, a long way down, he saw something that gave him heart. There, strong and untroubled by the swirling flood, stood Redgum. If he could only get to Redgum he would be safe. Nothing could shift him.

Then he saw something else. Flying above him, through the branches, was Gleam, looking for something, it seemed.

"Gleam! Gleam!" Spindles yelled at the top of his voice.

"Spindles! There you are!" answered Gleam. "I've been looking for you everywhere. Hippie thought you might be stranded."

"Good old Hippie!" said Spindles. Then he called, "Gleam! What can I do? How can I get out?"

"Do what I tell you," answered the galah. "From up here I can see where there are rocks you can climb and sand bars that haven't been washed away. I'll lead you."

Spindles was still sobbing, but he wiped his arm across his nose, sniffed, and tried to listen to what Gleam was telling him.

"Spindles!" It was Gleam talking again.

"Yes, Gleam?"

"Can you see that large rock on the other side of the branch you are holding?"

"Yes, I think so."

"Well, climb over the branch, and try to jump to the rock."

"I'll try."

So Spindles climbed up on to the branch. It did not feel very safe, and it moved a bit under his weight. He stood there, balancing.

"I can't do it!" he cried.

"Of course you can," Gleam assured him.

And when Spindles saw the bright pink of Gleam's feathers against the sullen grey of the sky, it seemed to cheer him somehow. He remembered how the galahs were something like the Bethlehem angels in the sky. And, in his heart, he prayed, "Help me, Jesus. Please."

Again, he took a deep breath, and jumped. His right foot landed safely. His left foot, the one with no shoe, landed on a sharp point that made him cry out with pain. He dropped down on all fours—but he stayed there.

"Good work. Well done!" said Gleam. "Now, there's a kind of sand bar just in front of you. It's covered in water, but it's not very deep. Go for that."

And Spindles did and he was all right.

And so he jumped to another branch and then to another sand bar. From there to a rock.

From the rock to another. From this rock to a branch. And so on.

It took an hour, but finally, he was close to Redgum. And the nearer he got, the more unhappy he became.

You see, he was pleased to be safe. But he was also afraid of what Redgum would say. For during the last hour, Spindles had been thinking while he climbed. Hippie had told him not to break the Bush Law. And Redgum had heard him. And Spindles had seemed so cocky about it. After what happened to Joey, there was just no excuse for Spindles. At least Joey could blame the dingo. Spindles couldn't blame anyone!

Spindles stood balanced on a rock. Between him and Redgum there was nothing but water—about two metres wide and a metre deep, and moving fast. Beneath the water, somewhere, was one of Redgum's roots.

"Climb on to the root and you'll be all right," squawked Gleam, who was now sitting on a low branch of the great tree.

"But I can't see it," moaned Spindles.

"Neither can I," answered Gleam. "The water's too muddy now. But it's there somewhere."

"How can you jump on to something you can't see?" objected Spindles.

"You have to take my word for it, Spins," answered Gleam. "I know it's there."

"And I know it's there, too," said the deep voice of Redgum. "Believe my word and you will be safe."

"All right, I'll do it," whispered Spindles. "Where exactly is it?"

"It's about half a metre directly in front of you," Gleam answered.

"If you take a big step in front of you into the water, you'll be standing on it. It should be only about ten centimetres under the water. Don't you remember it?"

"I've never had to use it before," groaned Spindles.

Nevertheless, he tried. He took a big step. If he missed he would fall and possibly drown! He only had someone else's word to go on. But, after all, it was Redgum's word. He could be trusted, surely. And just when Spindles thought he had missed, and that he really was going to tumble into the water again, his foot felt something firm and strong. It was there after all. Soon, both feet and both hands were gripping the root (he was so wet it didn't matter any more), and he was crawling towards the big tree.

In a minute he was safe, sitting thankfully on one of the low branches of the tree, with Gleam alongside him.

"I say, old chap, are you all right?" came Hippie's voice from about twenty metres away, on the bank of the creek.

"Yes, I'm all right, Hippie," Spindles answered. "Bit wet and sore, that's all." And he was very tired, too.

"Didn't know you were so keen on swimming," shouted Hippie.

But Spindles wasn't in a laughing mood, and said nothing. So Hippie, happy that he was safe, said no more.

Spindles didn't know what to do next. He could not get away, but he couldn't stay in the tree all night, either.

"Redgum?" he asked timidly.

"Yes, Spindles?"

"What shall I do now?"

"Nothing."

"But I can't stay here!"

There was no answer, and Spindles knew Redgum well enough not to keep on chattering. When Redgum was ready, he would say anything else he had to say.

But then Spindles remembered something else.

"Redgum?"

There was still no answer, but he continued.

"Redgum, I am sorry I caused all this trouble. It was my fault. I knew that the Law of the Bush said to keep to high ground but—"

"You thought you knew better."

"Yes, I suppose I did."

"It's a good thing there's a higher Law, Spindles."

"A higher Law?"

"Yes. It's called the Law of Love. It says that even when people do wrong, you can still love them and still help them. If they will trust you, of course. You trusted us. You did what we said. And we were able to help you. And so you've learned something else, Spindles."

"Yes, I have."

"And here's another verse from the Bible for you to think about:

For God so loved the world that he gave his only Son, that whoever believes in him should not perish but have eternal life.
(John 3:16)

"God saves people because He loves them."

There was silence again.

Spindles still found it hard to really understand why Jesus had come to the world. But it was becoming clearer. He could understand love, anyway. And there was something about the strength and safety of Redgum that reassured him and took away all his fear. Perhaps God was like that.

But Spindles still didn't know how he was going to get home. It was growing darker, and soon it would be night time. He was starting to shiver. His broken skin was stinging and his bruised body was aching. He couldn't stay in the tree all night.

But then he remembered that Redgum was not the only one who loved him. And nor was Gleam. Or Hippie. Or Roo. His mum and dad loved him too. They would come and look for him.

And sure enough, before long, he heard the sound of the four-wheel-drive vehicle that his dad drove. And soon Dad was wading through the creek calling him. And soon he was in his dad's strong arms. And soon he was home, bathed, fed and tucked in bed.

Most of all, he knew that no matter what happened there was always someone who loved him.

It was easy to go to sleep knowing that.

5

Spindles and the Numbat

Spindles and Hippie were having a contest.

Hippie started it, as usual. He and Spindles had been wandering through the bush when Hippie had suddenly stopped and said, "I'll take this track and you take that branch."

Spindles had looked for a branch track, but of course there was no such thing. What was there in fact was a branch—a real branch from a tree.

"Ha, ha, ha," responded Spindles. "I'll *bow* to that one."

"I thought you'd *twig* it," replied Hippie.

"You can't *leaf* me behind."

"But I can get to the *root* of the matter."

"Not if you're *barking* up the wrong tree."

"Don't worry, I *stick* to the point."

"I think you beat around the *bush*."

"Isn't it time we *scrubbed* this business?"

Spindles didn't want to be outdone. So he thought desperately for one last pun. At last he got it.

"I *wood* if I could," he said.

But Hippie still had the final word. "I really can't think of any more, old chap," he said. "I'm *stumped.*"

It was one of those delightful, sunny mornings in the outback when the heat of the day had not yet become uncomfortable. The air was clear and crisp, the breeze was cool, and the blue of the sky was like a great, deep pool into which you wanted to dive and disappear for ever.

Even the grey-green of the mountain bush foliage was colourful this morning. The acacia trees and the mulga scrub seemed almost fresh. And the black stumps of the grass trees (Spindles called them "yackas") stood out boldly against the grey foliage and the brown earth. And there was, of course, the ever-present spinifex, prickly, yellow, and yet still somehow better than the plain brown earth and the grey rocks.

Along the creek bed stood, as they had stood, it seemed, forever, the huge redgums, their long roots burrowing deep into the earth, searching out the dampness that lay far beneath the surface. And from it they drew life.

Hippie and Spindles were not alone. It was the kind of morning on which friends could easily get together. The galahs were squawking from tree to tree, like colored rags blown about by the wind. Roo and Joey were feeding a few metres away. Tank, the goanna, was stretched out on a rock, so that it was hard to see which was which—until you looked into his sharp eyes. And somewhere far above, a wedgetailed eagle hung in the sky, ominous, but not dangerous.

The creek had worn its way through rocks over the years, carving a deep slice into a cliff on its western side, so that the face of the rock wall rose sheer for well over twenty-five metres. Over the top hung a few shaggy pieces of grass and bush. And behind them again stretched the Dusty Range. On the eastern side slow hills drifted up to the peaks of the Range. And just south of where Spindles and Hippie were, was the crossing where the homestead track forded the creek. There stood Redgum, master of the Range.

Spindles sat down to rest a while, chewing a bit of grass and leaning against a convenient rock. Hippie stood nearby.

Roo hopped over, followed by Joey, who was now nearly as big as his mother.

"Good morning, Spindles," she began politely.

"Morning, Roo."

"My leg's nearly perfect again, Spins!" It was Joey talking now, and like all children, he could never see the point in wasting time by using "good mornings" or "good afternoons." If you liked someone why couldn't you just talk to them? Did you have to be introduced all over again? So Joey plunged straight into his subject. And holding out his hind leg he showed Spindles where the wound had been.

"Look! You can't even see where it was now. The fur has grown right over it."

"Gee, so it has," agreed Spindles. "That's good."

And he remembered how Joey had nearly died, except that he had saved him. And that reminded him of something he had been meaning to ask Roo.

"Roo."

"Yes, Spindles?" came her soft reply.

"You remember how Redgum told me that when I found Joey it was something like Jesus finding me?"

"Yes, child, I remember very well."

"Well, I still don't get it, really. What happens to me when he finds me? What sort of things does he do to me?"

"Well, Spindles, it's like this. Your life on earth is not the only life you can have. You can live forever in heaven—"

"But how? How do you get there? Do you have to die first? Will there be animals there? Will you be there?"

"One thing at a time, please! Yes, I'll be there. God has promised that animals will be in his Kingdom. And you can be there, too, if you let Jesus into your life."

"But that's the bit I don't understand."

"Well, Spins, I'm not sure that I understand it either. But I do know—"

Suddenly Roo was interrupted by Hippie.

"What Roo is trying to say, old chap, is that it's all rather a mystery, you know, but one thing's perfectly clear. If you want to live forever in heaven, you've got to trust Jesus."

"Yeah, that's right," came a slow, low voice. It was Tank. "You can't get there without him, because he's the only one who can get you ready."

"What do you mean by that?" asked poor Spindles, more bewildered than ever. And no doubt he would have become even more confused if something hadn't happened to catch everyone's attention.

Gleam came streaking from the sky.

"Hey! Everyone! Come and see what I've found! I've never seen one in my life before. It's got a bushy tail, like a dingo. And stripes like a painted aborigine. I don't know what it is! It's over here."

"I say, steady on, old chap," answered Hippie. "What is it? Animal, vegetable or mineral?"

"This is no time for games, Hippie," Gleam squawked severely. "It's a matter of life and death! Follow me! Quickly!"

And with that, he rocketed into the air, screeched loudly, flapped his wings like leaves in a willy-willy, and again shouted, "Come on!"

It was obvious that Gleam had found something unusual. So the others followed as quickly as they could. Spindles untethered his pony and hopped on, Hippie swayed alongside him, and Roo and Joey hopped powerfully, but not hurriedly, just in front. Even Tank eased himself off his rock and, head erect, glided over the ground like a grey shadow.

Gleam led them down from the hills to the crossing, along the track, and about two kilometres towards the homestead.

It was hotter out there, for there was hardly any scrub, and the grass did nothing to temper the sun's heat, even for small animals.

Then Gleam fluttered to the earth, joined by a few of his companions. It looked as though a garden of pink and grey flowers had just bloomed.

There in front of them was the strangest little creature that they had ever seen. Spindles dropped from his pony and bent down to look closer. Hippie's long neck stretched downwards. Roo and Joey hopped close in. Tank stuck his head between Hippie's legs. Hippie saw him from the corner of his eye, turned his head so they were face to face and muttered, "Well, fancy meeting you here! What a coincidence."

But as Tank was not amused, he turned around and again looked at the little animal that stood before them. It was about the size of a large rat. It was fur covered, with four legs and a tail, and a pointed snout. It was reddish-brown in colour—on the front half, that is. The back half of the body was striped with white, giving it a zebra-like appearance. And its tail was long and velvety. Its bright little eyes looked very tired. And, thought Spindles, a little frightened.

It was Roo who spoke first, which was perhaps just as well, for her voice was soft and kind.

"Well, well, little chap. What are you? And what are you doing here?"

There was no answer. The small creature was obviously even more tired and frightened than it looked.

"You can talk to me," Roo went on. "We are all friends. We won't hurt you. Tell us, now. Who are you?"

His tiny eyes looked from Roo to Hippie to Spindles to Tank to Gleam—and then back again to Tank. He was worried about Tank.

"Don't be afraid of Tank. He won't hurt you," Roo assured him. "He's very kind really. Now, tell me, who are you?"

"I'm—I'm a—I'm a numbat," he said. "And I'm lost, and I'm hot and I don't know what to do."

"A numbat? What in the world is a numbat?"

This of course was Hippie, not Roo. For in spite of his culture, Hippie was not always as polite as he might have been. And he turned to Spindles.

"Have you ever heard of a numbat, Spins? I wonder if it's a cross between a numbskull and a wombat?"

"Hippie! Do be quiet!" demanded Roo.

And she continued talking to the little animal before her. "Don't you take any notice of Hippie. He's a nice fellow really." She paused and then went on, "You are a numbat? Is that right?"

"Yes," came the small voice's reply.

"Well, I'm afraid that none of us has ever seen a numbat before. So you'd better tell us a bit about yourself."

"Well, all right." And the numbat looked around at all the animals (who looked so huge to him) and tried to talk. But before he could say much, Spindles said, "Don't you think we ought to take him into a shady spot first?"

"Of course," answered Roo. "Of course we should."

So they all returned to the creek, gave him a drink, and sat down in a shady spot near Redgum. Then the little numbat told his story.

"I am a numbat. I have two brothers and one sister, and my name is Percival."

"But what is a numbat, Percival?" asked Spindles. And as he said "Percival," he knew that he wouldn't say it again. He would just call the numbat "Numbat."

"A numbat is a marsupial which lives on ants," Numbat replied, as if he was quoting from an encyclopedia. "Preferably termites."

"Termites!" exclaimed Spindles. "Ugh!"

"Oh, they taste succulent!" continued Numbat, licking his lips. "I find them in rotting logs, damp holes and old tree trunks. With my long nose and my very long tongue, I can root them out easily."

And he gave a demonstration of his ability, by shooting his tongue out in front of him and nicking a tiny bush ant from the ground about twenty centimetres away. It was gone in a moment and Numbat looked faintly pleased.

"But how did you get here?" demanded Roo.

"Well," answered Numbat, "I came from Western Australia and—"

"Western Australia!" said Spindles.

"Western Australia!" said Hippie.

"Yes, that's right. The numbat is the official mammal symbol of Western Australia."

"Even I couldn't make it here from Western Australia, you know," protested Hippie.

"Oh, I didn't walk!" continued Numbat. "You see, there are many trees where I live, and trucks often come into the area to load up with wood. A few days ago, I was inside a very large log searching for termites when the log was grabbed by some men, and winched on to their truck. I tried to escape, but the hole I had entered was covered by a huge chain. And when the log was loaded, the hole was blocked by another log. I was imprisoned.

"I didn't know what to do. I felt the truck moving and I desperately wanted to get off. But there was no way. It was dark and bumpy and I had no idea where we were going. Fortunately, there were plenty of termites, so I didn't go hungry."

"What about drink?" asked Roo, thoughtfully.

"That was a real problem. After a day and a half I was parched. I thought I would go mad. But that day a thunder storm broke, and water dribbled over the sides of the tree trunks right into the hole where I was. Soon it was full of water. It was uncomfortable, but I don't mind

damp places, and it was lovely not to be
thirsty.

"Then, yesterday, I noticed that the logs
had shifted a bit. I could see light through the
entrance to the hole. I tried to escape, but
while the truck was moving, the logs rubbed
against each other, and I was nearly squashed
to death between them. So I waited till
nightfall, when the truck stopped. Then I
squeezed out of the hole and looked around.
Nothing looked familiar. So I climbed down
from the truck to explore. I wandered back
down the road, and found a track. I thought it
might lead to a house, so I followed it, and that
was where you (and he looked towards Gleam)
saw me this morning."

"Well, you're safe now, old fellow," said
Hippie. "And you needn't worry any more. You
can stay here with us, you know. Jolly fine
idea, really."

"Stay here?" answered Numbat. "I couldn't
do that. I think I'd die. I'd miss my family. And
it's really too hot. How do you survive in a hot
place like this?"

"Hot? Nothin' like it. Dunno how you can
stand the cold. Give me 'ot weather any day."
Thus spoke Tank, who thrived on the heat.

"It might be all right for you, Tank,"
answered Numbat. "But I think it would kill me.

Furthermore, how many termites have you got here? I can eat up to 20,000 a day, you know."

"20,000 a day!" echoed Spindles, incredulously. But Numbat was still talking.

"Anyway, we can only live with our own families. Do you know that no one has ever raised a numbat in a zoo? We die if we're not in the right place."

Once again, the little creature sounded very learned. It seemed strange to the others that he was so proud of being a numbat, when he was so small and so unusual.

"I've got to get home again. I'll die if I don't."

The animals all talked among themselves to see what they could think of. But no one seemed to know what to do. When they all stopped chattering, and seemed to have nothing else to suggest, Redgum spoke.

"Little Numbat, don't be afraid. Everything will work out. Spindles will help you to get home."

Spindles jumped up as suddenly as if he had just sat down on a patch of spinifex. Redgum continued speaking, but this time to Spindles.

"You must see that Numbat is put on a truck that will take him back to his home. It is up to you, Spindles."

The great tree stood silent.

When Spindles got home that night, there was an unusual bump under his shirt. But no one noticed, and before long, Percival the Numbat was safely in a box under Spindles' bed. Spindles lay in bed for a long time that night wondering what to do with Numbat. He couldn't think of anything. Slowly, he became drowsy. His eyes dropped and he was nearly asleep when he thought he heard someone say something about "the West."

He hopped out of bed and crept to his door where he could hear what was going on in the lounge. There was his dad talking to his mum, and to Butch, the station hand!

What's Butch doing in the house? Spindles asked himself in amazement.

"Better take the last lot of wool to the West," his dad was saying. "Prices down South aren't too good. Perhaps they'll be better over there."

"When'll I start?" growled Butch.

"First light, Butch," Spindles' dad replied.

And Butch drifted out of the room.

First light! thought Spindles. *I've got to get Numbat on that truck.*

Spindles didn't sleep much that night.

He mustn't sleep in. He must be awake early.

Before the sun had risen, Spindles crept from his room. Numbat was tucked inside his

pajama coat. He moved silently to the back door and peeped out. No one in sight. Across the house yard towards the shearing shed he could see the outline of the truck. It was already loaded. A light in the stockmen's quarters showed that Butch was inside. Spindles darted to the truck and sprang on to the tray. He clung to a rope holding the wood bales in place, and looked desperately for somewhere to hide Numbat. The bales were so tightly packed that it seemed impossible. He clambered to the top and crawled around there. There was a sharp noise from the men's quarters, and he froze. But Butch was still inside. So he kept searching. In the pre-dawn darkness it was hard to see anything clearly.

Numbat stuck his nose out of Spindles' pajamas. "Can you find anything?" he whispered.

"Not yet," answered Spindles.

"Let me look," suggested Numbat.

He crawled over the whole load until he was right against the cabin of the truck.

"Hey! Here's something!" he said.

There, between two bales and the cabin was a spot just big enough for a numbat.

"Hop in there!" Spindles urged him. And the little animal sprang down into the darkness between the bales.

"This is fine!" he told Spindles.

In a moment, Spindles was gone. A half a minute later he was back with a couple of tins. One contained water. The other was full of dead termites. Numbat turned up his long nose.

"Live ones taste nicer," he mumbled.

"Sorry," answered Spindles. "But live ones wouldn't stay there. Besides, you ought to be grateful that we all helped catch them for you."

"I know. I am grateful. But I still prefer live ones."

"Well, I hope you'll be comfortable. And I hope you can find your home again."

"I'll do my best," answered Numbat.

"We'll be praying for you."

"I know you will. I'm counting on it."

Suddenly the light went off in the men's quarters, and Butch appeared at the door, latching it, with his back to the truck. Spindles dived off the opposite side and fled back to the house.

"I wonder if Numbat got home safely," Spindles asked later of no one in particular.

"Of course he did," said Roo. "We prayed didn't we?"

"Yes, we did."

"I wish he could have stayed here," Spindles went on.

"You know very well he couldn't stay here, old chap," said Hippie. "He would have died away from his home."

"He might've got used to it," argued Spindles.

"Impossible!"

"But why?"

"I can't understand it either," grumbled Tank. "I just love it 'ere. Beautiful."

It was then that Redgum joined the discussion.

"The reason that Numbat couldn't stay here is the same reason that you can't go to heaven—not as you are, anyway. You see, numbats are made for forest country where there are plenty of termites, and where they have the companionship of their own kind.

"And you are a creature of earth. Unless you are changed by the Lord Jesus Christ, you can't survive in heaven. If you went there as you are you wouldn't like it anyway!"

"Heaven? I wouldn't like heaven?" interrupted Spindles.

The animals were surprised that Spindles dared to interrupt Redgum. But the big tree simply continued, "Not even heaven. That's why Jesus said you have to be born again to enter the kingdom of heaven. Only when he gives you a new nature can you be happy—even in heaven. That's why you must invite him into your life."

Redgum had finished. The animals were silent. And Spindles was thoughtful.

He said to himself, *If we prayed for the Lord to get Numbat safely to his home, perhaps I could pray for the Lord to get me safely home to heaven?*

And as he looked towards Redgum, he fancied he heard the great tree speak again. For with his arms uplifted, and pointing heavenwards, he seemed to be saying, "Father, another child is being born into your kingdom. I commit him to you. For I know you will receive him."

And somewhere a long way off, a little numbat was singing to himself as he bounced along on the back of a truck. He seemed to know that God would take care of him too.

6

Spindles Climbs a Cliff

"Dad, why don't we ever go to church?" asked
Spindles.

"How can we, when we live way out here?"
his dad replied testily.

"Oh, I don't mean that," said Spindles. "What I
mean is, even when we go to the city for a while,
we never go to church. And the minister never
calls in here when he visits the other stations."

"Now, don't you start preaching to me," his
dad answered smartly. "When I need church,
I'll say so. In the meantime I can get on quite
well. And I don't want to hear any more from
you on the subject. Do you understand?"

"Yes, Dad," murmured Spindles. But he
wasn't very pleased. He wasn't preaching to his
father. He only wanted to know. But he had to
admit that his dad was doing pretty well
whether he went to church or not. Perhaps he
really didn't need God. But then, even Redgum

seemed to need God. And if he prayed and asked the Lord for help, surely his father and mother could do the same—sometimes anyway.

Spindles finished his breakfast, wiped his sleeve over his mouth, and wandered out of the kitchen.

A couple of hours later, he was with his friends at the Dusty Range. The little kangaroo bounced up to him.

"Guess what, Spins," cried Joey. "There's a gang of rock climbers camped down the creek. They've got ropes and hooks and pegs and special boots and all sorts of things."

And all the while he was talking, Joey was jumping up and down with excitement, for this was something new to him.

Hippie was less enthusiastic, but even he couldn't conceal his interest.

"What a lot of gear just to climb a few hills," he declared. "Anyone would think the job was difficult. I mean to say, it's a piece of cake really, old chap."

"Can't understand what all the fuss's about," grunted Tank. "Disturbin' the peace and quiet. Blinkin' nuisances, if you ask me. And anyway, who needs ropes?"

And with that, he darted up to the top of a pile of rocks, like a vanishing shadow, just to show how easily it could be done.

Spindles, however, was fascinated by the prospect of watching the climbers in action, and he ran off to look for them.

"I say, where are you going, Spins?" shouted Hippie, but Spindles did not hear him, and did not answer. Joey hopped alongside of him, but when Spindles approached the people he held back and stayed in the shadow of some scrub.

There were two tents and three cars near where the first cliffs rose up by the side of the creek. The blue and orange of the canvas shone brightly against the grey-green of the gums and the ochre-red of the cliffs.

Four men and two women were sitting around a camp fire drinking tea.

"G'day, young fellow," one of the men said. "Where'd you spring from?"

"I live at the station over there," answered Spindles, indicating with a sweep of his hand the general direction of the homestead.

"What's your name?"

"Well, it's really Timothy. But everyone calls me Spindles."

"Spindles." The man spoke it thoughtfully and seemed to roll his tongue over it, as if he was tasting a new drink for the first time.

"Well, then, Spindles it will be. How'd you like a cuppa?"

"All right."

Spindles joined the group, and immediately began to ask them questions.

"What are you doing out here?"

"First of all, we'd better introduce ourselves. I'm Bert, this is Alf, and this is Ed and this is Rolf. And over here, Elaine and Julie."

Spindles nodded to them all, and again asked what they were doing.

Bert continued. "We've come here to do some rock climbing. It's our hobby, I guess you could say."

"But why come out here? Aren't there better mountains than these to climb? These aren't much—they're only hills, really."

"True. There are much higher cliff faces in the Blue Mountains. But they're very hard to get at. These are further from the city, but we can drive right to the foot of them, yet they're still very steep and difficult to climb."

Spindles had never thought of the Dusty Range as being a place for mountain climbers. But when he looked at the cliffs, he realised that they were rather steep.

"Look at those chimneys in the cliff face," Bert went on.

"What chimneys?" asked Spindles. He couldn't see any.

"Those deep crevices running from top to bottom," Bert continued. "We use them to climb up."

"They give us a foothold," added Ed. "And we can brace our backs against one side and our feet against the other so that we don't fall."

"Well, what about all these ropes and things?" asked Spindles.

"Come on, we'll show you."

So they all got up from the fire, made sure it was safe, and Bert and Ed began to assemble their gear.

About half an hour later, they were all at the foot of the cliff. So Spindles sat down to watch.

He didn't know it, but Hippie, Roo, Tank and Gleam were all hidden in the shadows of the trees also watching what was going on, although they didn't want Spindles to see them. Only Joey was in view, but still keeping his distance.

Ed and Bert began to climb. Initially, they had no trouble, and didn't use any of their equipment. Soon, however, they came to a very steep part, where the rock face was smooth, and there was little to hold on to. So Bert, who was leading, took out a piton, a metal spike about thirty centimetres long, and hammered it into a small crack in the rock. He

fastened a rope to the piton, a rope which was also tied around his waist. But he did not use the spike to support him. He still sought for hand grips—or more accurately, finger grips—in the rock surface, and for tiny ledges in which to place his toes. The piton was only to stop him, if perchance he fell.

Spindles watched amazed as Bert seemed to squeeze his finger tips into the rock itself and as his toes caught fast in cracks so small that Spindles couldn't even see them.

Soon he had edged himself up past the piton and he was searching with one hand on his belt for another spike, while the other hand held him secure. Again, he hammered the piton into the rock, then pulled down on it with all his force to make sure that it would hold. Satisfied, he tied the rope to it, and began to climb on.

Meanwhile below him, Ed reached the first piton. The same rope that joined Bert to the pitons, joined him also. But Ed now removed the spike and replaced it on his belt. Now they were past it, they didn't need it anymore.

And so they inched up the rock face, like two struggling insects, striving for the top. Spindles watched with subdued fascination, as the two men seemed to hang on the rock wall. Or they jammed themselves into the crevice, backs pressed against one wall, and feet thrust firmly against the other. The bright yellow shirt that Ed wore made it easy to see them from below, even when they were in shadow.

Spindles decided to go to the top to meet them. So he ran to the end of the hill, a run which took him almost down to the creek crossing, and then scampered up the back of the rise until he had reached the top. There he lay down, looked over the edge, and watched the two men below him gradually drawing closer to where he was. It took a long time, but eventually they were within a metre or so. Finally, Bert's head appeared over the top, followed by his body, and in a moment he was sitting alongside Spindles.

Down below him, Spindles' sharp eye could now make out the shadowy forms of the animals watching from the shelter of the trees. And not far away was the campfire, with the rest of the party now back there again preparing the lunch.

"Are you going to climb down again?" Spindles asked Bert.

"No fear," answered Bert, as he watched Ed removing the last of the pitons before he climbed over the top. Bert was holding the rope that Ed was now safe.

"Why not?"

"People are made to climb up, not down," was Bert's reply.

That's a strange thing to say, Spindles said to himself, but when he thought about it, he realised that he always found climbing up hills less dangerous than climbing down them: it required more energy, but you weren't nearly so likely to fall.

There was no more time for talk, as Ed was now mounting the cliff-edge, and both men were fully concentrating on this.

Soon they were walking back down the western slope of the hill, then north again along the creek to the camp.

Spindles had to go home to lunch, so he found his pony and headed off.

Next morning, he returned to the Range as early as he could. But as sharp as he was, he was too late to catch the climbers. They had made a prompt start and were already well up the cliff. All of them were climbing today, and they were scattered over the cliff face like bright spots of paint splashed there by some giant artist. Spindles recognised Ed's yellow shirt again. And he could pick out Elaine and Julie by the red blouses they wore. Each was climbing with one of the men and they were already ten metres up the cliff.

The animals had lost interest by now.

"Can't see any point to it, can you, Spins?" demanded Hippie. "I mean to say, old chap, why don't they just go round the back of the hill if they want to get to the top? Much easier."

"I dunno," said Tank. "If you want to get to the top, you might as well go straight up. But danged if I know why they 'ave all those ropes and stuff. Any goanna can scoot up there in no time."

"Why climb at all?" asked Gleam. And the cheeky galah immediately flapped his wings and rose to the top of the cliff without touching it once.

Roo wasn't even there. She had taken Joey over to the other side of the Range looking for some succulent grass and wouldn't be back for hours.

But Spindles was still fascinated by the climbers. And he wandered over towards the cliff.

He stopped at the bottom of one of the chimneys. From where he was, it looked easier to climb than he had thought.

I wonder if I could climb up there? he asked himself.

He looked around. There were no animals in sight now.

Perhaps he could climb a little, anyway. It wouldn't hurt. And if he got stuck, he could always climb down again. So he hoisted himself up. At first he found some quite good hand and footholds. His small fingers and toes fitted into the cracks in the rock more easily than those of the climbers.

This is a cinch, he said to himself. *I don't know why they need all those ropes and pegs.*

And he climbed a little higher.

He made himself secure and then looked up the chimney for a new finger-hold. He couldn't see anywhere to grip. He stretched upwards with his fingers, feeling around for a crack. Finally, the tips of his fingers on his left hand felt what appeared to be a tiny ledge. He shifted his foot slightly and stretched to his fullest extent. His fingers could just bend over to grip the small lip of rock. He wriggled them slightly, tested his grip, and then tried to move his feet up.

Without warning, they slipped!

He kicked desperately against the rock seeking a hold. His right foot dislodged a small stone which tumbled and bounced down into the creek bed. The strain on his fingers was almost too much to bear. He could feel his skin being cut by a sharp part of the rock. Frantically, he slid his feet up and down. Just when he thought he could hold no longer, his left foot found a hole. He jammed his toes into it and they held him. At last the pressure was removed from his tortured fingers; his right foot now found a grip and his right hand was able to take some of the pressure.

He could shift around a bit now, and he was able to push his back against one wall of the chimney and his feet against the other, so that he was held firm without effort.

He looked down.

He was only about ten metres up. But had he fallen, he could easily have broken an arm or a leg; certainly he would have been badly hurt.

Now the going was a bit easier. There were plenty of places to hang on to.

I guess if I were a bit taller I could have got over the last bit easily, Spindles said to himself. *But then again, my small fingers held on better than Bert's would have done, I bet.*

About five metres higher, Spindles again ran into trouble. There didn't seem to be anywhere to put his hands or feet at all. The chimney was becoming too narrow even for his small body. He knew that he would have to reach around it and climb out of it. He stretched his right arm outside the chimney. He found a prominent knob, easy and safe to hold. His right foot explored the area below his hand. A ledge was wide enough for him. So he began to clamber out. Soon he was out of the crevice and climbing up the cliff-face itself.

This was more difficult, but more exciting. Now he was really climbing. For a moment, he glanced down. There was nothing below him. He quickly looked up again.

There must be another chimney somewhere, he thought. *I'm sure I remember one just over to the right.*

He edged over in that direction. Once again, he had to reach to his fullest extent to find finger-holds. He walked his fingers up the rock, like big, white spiders seeking a resting place. His left hand found a slight bulge around which his fingers neatly fitted. His right hand just reached a small ledge over which his finger tips could fold.

Now for his feet. His arms were stretched so high he couldn't look down, so he had to feel his way again. Cautiously, he lifted his left foot. He scraped it upwards, feeling for a place to stand.

Nowhere!

So he found his former spot and shifted his right foot. Slowly he moved it round in every direction that he could reach.

Nowhere!

He was stuck!

The only thing to do was to climb down again. He moved his fingers back to their original positions.

Now he looked down to see where to go next. And as he did, a swift wave of fear broke across his heart. What if he couldn't get down?

Of course he would get down. He had got up here; there must be a way down. So he began to look for his earlier ledges and cracks. But reaching down for them was quite a different thing from reaching up for them.

Again, a cold gush of fear poured into his heart. What if he really couldn't get down?

And then he remembered what Bert had said to him the day before. "People are made to climb up, not down." Perhaps it was really true.

Once again he struggled to find toeholds so that he could lower himself. But somehow, no matter how far down he reached, the rock-face was too smooth to grip. There was one tiny jutting ledge just big enough for his big toe. But when he tested it, his foot slipped straight off. He tried again, but now the stone broke off in crumbles and splashed down the cliff in a tiny shower.

With terror, Spindles realised that he was trapped. There was no way that he could help himself.

"Hippie!" he shouted.

But Hippie was now far away.

"Tank! Roo!"

But again there was no answer.

"Bert! Ed! Help! Help me! I'm stuck!"

But the climbers were now far above him, and the range-winds carried Spindles' voice out over the creek and down into the trees.

Spindles called again and again, but to no avail. No one could hear him; no one could help him.

But there was one who did see and who did know. Fifteen metres below him, and a hundred metres east of the cliff, stood Redgum. And he could see the small, frightened boy clinging to the cliff like a shell-fish. But unlike a shell-fish, the boy could come unstuck only too easily. And Redgum knew that it was time to act.

There were some galahs sitting in his branches.

"Call Gleam," said Redgum.

Immediately, the galahs lifted into the air and went squawking in search of Gleam. It seemed only moments before they had returned with him. And it was only a moment again before he knew the situation.

Meanwhile, Ed and Bert had both finished their climb and were sitting at the top of the cliff waiting for the others.

"Hey! What do you think you're doing?" spluttered Bert.

For Gleam had suddenly appeared out of
the blue and was flapping his wings around
Bert's head and squawking loudly. What he
was saying was, "Quick! Come and help
Spindles! He's stuck on the cliff." But all that
Bert heard was loud squawking. And Gleam
knew it. Most adults were far too proud to
understand animal-talk. So Gleam was
prepared to use other methods.

He dropped to the ground a few feet from
the two men, and began to limp downhill.

"Well, look at that," said Ed, amazed.

"I'll see if I can grab 'im," answered Bert.

So he rose to his feet and strode toward the
bird. But as soon as he did, Gleam fluttered a
few yards further on. Again, Bert approached
him and bent down to try to pick him up. And
again, Gleam fluttered just out of reach.

Ed laughed aloud.

"Nice bird catcher you are!" he exclaimed.
"Let me show you how to do it."

But Ed had no more success than Bert.
Every time he thought he had Gleam in his
hands, the pink and grey galah slipped a few
feet in front of him.

"You know, I think that bird's leading us
on," laughed Bert. "He sure doesn't want to be
caught—but he doesn't want to get away,
either."

"I wonder if he's trying to show us something," Ed suggested.

"Come off it," said Bert. "No galah is that smart."

"I dunno, Bert. You'd be surprised. Let's follow him anyway."

"Okay, Ed. We've got to go down sooner or later. Might as well follow him."

When Gleam heard this, he flew further on, dropped to the ground, and waited for the men to catch up again. And so they went on, the galah keeping just in front of them.

They reached the bottom of the cliff and Gleam led them up the creek to the spot where Spindles had started to climb. And then, he flew up level with the boy and hovered there. Spindles was just able to turn his head enough to see him.

"Gleam! Am I glad to see you! Help me!"

"That's why I'm here, Spins," answered Gleam. "Redgum saw you, and sent me to help. Ed and Bert are just below. They'll get you down."

But the shape of the cliff was such that from where they stood, they couldn't see the boy at all!

"I guess that bird was having us on after all," remarked Bert. "Might as well go back to camp."

"Yeah. Looks like there are three galahs here, not one," laughed Ed.

So the men shrugged their shoulders and wandered off.

When Gleam looked down and saw them going back to the camp, he screeched frantically and flew towards them again, flapping his wings and squawking loudly.

"Strike, here he is again," said Bert. And he turned round to look at Gleam. As he did, he caught a glimpse of a spot of colour on the cliff.

"Hey, one of the fellers is climbing down again," he cried.

"Hang on—that's not one of us. It's that kid. What's his name again . . . ?"

"Brindle or something, wasn't it?"

"No, not Brindle. Something like that . . . er . . . Spindles. That's it! It's that kid, Spindles. He must have tried to follow us."

And even from where they were, they could see his fair hair and his skinny white legs pointing down like two pieces of spaghetti from his small body.

"Well, looks like we've got some more climbing to do, Bert. That kid needs help."

They ran to the foot of the cliff and it seemed only moments until the two men were climbing towards Spindles. He couldn't see them, but he could hear the clanking of the pitons and rope-hooks on their belts as they climbed; and Gleam was hovering near to him, encouraging him.

"Don't worry, Spins. There's help coming. Bert and Ed are on their way. Hang on. You'll be right."

"They'd better hurry," answered Spindles. "I don't know how much longer I can hold."

And his fingers were white with pressure, and his toes had lost all feeling. His shoulders were aching and his skin was beginning to feel the heat of the strengthening sun.

Soon he could hear Bert's voice. "Hang on, kid. We'll soon be there."

There was the sound of banging, as pitons were driven into the rock, and then, out of the corner of his eye, Spindles saw Bert emerging from the chimney. It was the most welcome sight he had seen for a long time.

Slowly, Bert moved across the cliff, carefully placing spikes as he came. Ed was behind him and they were both joined by rope. Then, he was alongside of the boy and had his strong arm around his shoulders. He supported Spindles while he eased him back down to the edge of the chimney. From there, with the help of the rope, Spindles was able to clamber into the chimney and then fairly easily down to the ground.

By this time, the animals had heard about the adventure, and were all standing back among the trees again, watching what was happening.

Spindles was very shaken. He had had a bad fright and it took him a while to recover. The climbers gave him another cup of tea and helped him to calm down.

As it was now well into the afternoon, and Spindles had been expected home for lunch, it was no surprise that his father turned up in the station jeep looking for him. The story was soon told and Spindles' dad hardly knew how to express his gratitude to Ed and Bert.

"Actually, you ought to thank that galah, you know," said Ed. "Strange thing that. That bird really seemed to know that Spindles was caught on the cliff. Wonder how he did it?"

"Pure coincidence, Ed," said Bert. "Galahs are smart, but not that smart."

Gleam, who had been quite pleased to hear Ed's comments, suddenly became offended and flew right over Bert's head, screeching his loudest.

"There you are!" laughed Ed. "He heard you!"

"Well, galah or no galah," added Spindles' father, "I appreciate what you did. Spindles is pretty self-sufficient and he can normally look after himself quite well. But I'm sure glad to know that when he needed help, there was someone around who could help him."

"No problem at all, Mr. Thornton," answered Ed. "In fact, I find life to be a bit like that. I'm pretty self-sufficient, too, but I'm always glad to know that when I need help, there's someone to help me, too."

"Uh? What do you mean?"

"I'm talking about God, Mr. Thornton," laughed Ed. "It's good to know he's around when you need him."

"Oh, yes, of course. Well, anyway, thanks again for what you did. You don't know how much I appreciate it."

And he grabbed Spindles and headed for home.

But as they were driving home, he said, "Spindles, you remember how you asked me yesterday about going to church?"

"Yes, Dad."

"I reckon we might do that next time we go to town."

"Gee, Dad, that'd be beaut."

Nothing more was said, but Spindles was inwardly very pleased.

Next time he was out at the Dusty Range, Spindles had a question for Redgum.

"Redgum."

"Yes, Spindles?"

"You saw me when I was stuck on the cliff, didn't you?"

"Yes, I did."

"Well, you must have seen me when I started climbing, too?"

"Yes, I did."

"Well, why didn't you stop me before I got stranded?"

"Two reasons, Spindles. First of all, the fact that you had to be helped showed your dad that he needed help, too, didn't it? And now you'll be going to church sometimes. Isn't that right?"

"Yes, Redgum. That's right."

"If I had stopped you too soon, that never would have happened. And secondly, you had to learn something else about life. People are made to go up, not down—"

"That's what Bert said," interrupted Spindles, without realising what he was doing.

"People are made to go up, not down," repeated Redgum, "and people are made to go to heaven, not hell. But you can't go up alone, and you can't go up unless you're properly prepared.

"Remember what the Lord Jesus Christ said in John 14:6: 'I am the way and the truth and the life; no one comes to the Father except through me.'"

"I don't think I'll ever forget that now," said Spindles. "I've got too good a reason to remember!"

7

Spindles and the Bandicoot

It was Easter time, and Spindles'
Correspondence School lessons had told him
something about the Easter Story.

Jesus Christ had been crucified, buried and
then raised from the dead. But although his
family was now attending church when they
went to town, Spindles' mother still seemed
doubtful about the resurrection of Jesus Christ.

"I think it really only means that *belief* in
Jesus lived on," she said, when she was going
through Spindles' lessons with him. "He
couldn't have really risen from the dead
himself. That's impossible. And anyway,
there's no scientific proof of it."

Spindles' mother didn't know anything
about science, but she had a high regard for it.
To say there was or wasn't scientific proof of
something was the end of the matter. If
"science" said something, she believed it.

"There must be some proof . . ." began
Spindles. But he didn't get any further.

"Don't you argue with me," said his mother.
"There's no more proof that Jesus Christ rose
from the dead than that—that—that there are
desert bandicoots left in the Dusty Range out
there. You find me a desert bandicoot and I
might believe in the resurrection!"

Desert bandicoots had in fact once lived in
the Dusty Range, but no one had seen one for
over twenty years now. A band of biologists
had even come looking for them about five
years previously. But after two weeks of
intensive study, they had concluded that the
species was extinct.

Spindles had heard about this, and had
often wished that he could find a bandicoot and
prove them all wrong. But, of course, he never
had. Now his mum's challenge stirred him up
and again he hoped he would find one. But he
knew that it was probably just a dream. The
desert bandicoot just didn't exist any more.

In his heart, of course, he knew that Jesus
Christ was alive. He knew that he had risen
from the dead. And so did Redgum and Roo
and Hippie and all his other friends. If only his
mum would believe too.

Anyway, today was Easter Saturday, and he
was out at the Dusty Range.

"G'day, Spins," Hippie greeted him.

"G'day, Hippie," answered Spindles.

"Did you hear about the man who tried to talk to his cat?" Hippie asked.

"No."

"Well, the man said, 'Talk to me, Puss,' and the cat answered, 'Me? 'Ow?'"

"Oh, that was a *paw* joke," answered Spindles.

"It was *fur* better than yours, anyway."

"I hope you won't *dog* me with remarks like that."

"I think we'd better give this up before we *hound* one another to death."

"Okay, you win," said Spindles. "What shall we do today?"

"Let's just go for a ramble over the hills," Hippie suggested. And so they did.

Joey hopped along, too, and even Tank accompanied them. Gleam and a few of the galahs were already fluttering around the hilltops.

They climbed the easy hills on the eastern side of the creek, with the sheer cliffs of the western wall of the gorge on their left. As they climbed higher, the breeze could be felt more strongly. The first coolness of autumn was tingeing the air, but it was overcome by the pleasing morning warmth of the uninterrupted sun. It was the kind of morning that made you want to climb high, to jump up and down, to sing, to run for the joy of running, to be yourself, free and alive and unconcerned with responsibility or care. Such a morning in the Australian Outback has to be experienced to be believed.

Spindles loved it. It was so clear, so bright, so free, so pure. "If heaven is like anything, it must be like this," he thought.

And he burst into a bouncing run, up the hill, striving for the top, just for the pleasure of being there. Hippie and Tank easily outran him, of course, and he was puffing much more than they when he arrived. He flung himself down on the ground, in spite of its prickles and small, sharp stones, and lay looking up at the endless blue of the sky. He wanted to swim in it.

After a while, he spoke to the others, "Have any of you ever seen a desert bandicoot?"

"Desert bandicoot? I say, old chap, they don't live here anymore," said Hippie. "The last person I know who saw one was my Uncle Cecil's great grandfather, and I wouldn't believe everything he said, anyway. Bit of a tale-teller, you know."

"Strike, Spins, a desert bandicoot?" exclaimed Tank. "What do you want one of them for? They're useless creatures. Stone the crows, we don't want them back here again. Never give a bloke a moment's peace."

"How do you know if you've never seen one?" Spindles asked.

"Well, I've never seen a desert bandicoot. But I know bandicoots. And they're all the same. Pugnacious little beggars."

"What do you mean?"

"Oh, the little blighters always want to fight. Stand up on their hind legs like blinkin' kangaroos and lash out at each other, they do. Then they jump into the air and try to scratch each other's eyes out—and anyone else's for that matter. You can keep 'em."

"Gee, I thought they were friendly little chaps," said Joey. "Like Numbat."

"Well, they look friendly," said Hippie. "Or so I believe. Rather like rabbits, except for their pointy noses. In fact, if you can imagine a mouse as big as a rabbit, you've got a bandicoot. And I wouldn't take too much notice of Tank, you know. They're not as bad as all that. Rather pleasant chaps, they say."

"That's all right for you, Hippie," answered Tank. "You're acting the goat yourself, half the time. You ought to get on well with bandicoots. Fair dinkum, sometimes I think *you're* an overgrown bandicoot—except you've got feathers instead of fur."

With that, Tank was off like a bullet—and just as well, too, for Hippie was close on his heels. But neither of them were really serious, and after a while they returned puffing and still insulting each other, but all in fun.

"Anyway, Spins, why in the world do you want a desert bandicoot?" This time it was Joey who asked the question. "Haven't you got enough friends?"

"Sure I have," Spindles answered. "I just wondered. That's all."

The time passed quickly, and it was time for Spindles to go home. So he found his pony, mounted him, and turned for the homestead.

That night, after tea, he saw Lonely sitting outside his door. He drifted over to him.

"Lonely."

"Yeah?"

"Have you ever seen a desert bandicoot?"

"Nope."

"Are there any around here now?"

"Nope."

"Do you know where there are any at all?"

"Nope."

And Lonely went on sitting, while his dog, Sleepy, went on sleeping, lying still at his feet.

Spindles was not put off. He was quite used to the boundary rider having very little to say.

So he waited a while. Then he thought of another question.

"Lonely, do you know where any used to be?"

"Well, yeah, I guess I do."

Again Spindles waited. He was longing to say, "Well for goodness' sake, tell me where." But he knew that you couldn't hurry Lonely. So he said, "I don't suppose you could show me the place?"

"I dunno. S'pose I could."

"When, Lonely?"

"Well, I've got to go out that way on Monday mornin'. I suppose I could show you then."

"Beauty!" answered Spindles. "I'll come with you."

And Spindles was pleased that Lonely didn't worry much about holidays, for otherwise he wouldn't have gone till Tuesday, and then Spindles would have been home doing schoolwork.

Early Monday morning, Spindles had his pony mounted, and was ready to go. He jogged alongside of Lonely, who was riding his motor bike as usual, with Sleepy in the box on the back, asleep as usual; and they headed for the Range.

This time they went around the back of the hills, on the northern side, away from the creek, where Spindles usually met his animal friends.

For a while they followed the track and then they turned in across country to the hills.

They followed a partly cleared area between the scrub. Lonely's bike bounced over the rough stones that were scattered over the surface, and he had to steer carefully to avoid the clumps of prickly spinifex. Occasionally a grass tree poked up among the bushes and a patch of scrub clung to the surface among the stones.

Soon the terrain became rougher and steeper, and the scrub began to thicken. Large rocky outcrops appeared, and it was in the shade of one of them that Lonely stopped his bike and muttered: "We'll 'ave to walk from here."

So Spindles also dismounted, and the two of them, and Sleepy, wandered on up the hill. The climb became even steeper now and both the rocks and the scrub increased in density. Above them, the hills rose up for hundreds of metres. They weren't much as mountains go, but they were tough enough when you were on foot.

After about twenty minutes, they approached some large sandstone rocks which rose sheer above them for about ten metres. They skirted around the side of them and

clambered to the top. There the surface was fairly level, but back in behind the rocks was a small cave. Like most caves in the outback, it was wide and shallow, but it did go deeper than most.

"Well, this is where they used ter be," said Lonely.

"Those museum blokes who came looking for bandicoots—did they come here?"

"Nope!"

"Didn't you tell them about this place?"

"Nope!"

"Why not, Lonely?"

"They never asked me."

Spindles was speechless. But that was Lonely. He was hardly what you'd call a good talker.

"Lonely, I think I'll stay here for a while and poke around. I can find my way home."

"All right," answered Lonely. "See you later." And he and Sleepy wandered off, leaving Spindles alone.

Spindles climbed into the cave. He looked into its furthest corners, lying on his stomach to do so. He crawled up and down its length. But he couldn't see any sign of life.

So he wandered out into the sunshine and sat down for a while to dream. The breeze was soothing and the sun was warm and he began to doze.

Suddenly, he sat up. Was that the voice of someone singing that he heard? No, there was only the sound of the breeze in the grass, whispering its everlasting song. And in the distance the screeching of a few white cockatoos.

He dozed off again.

There it was again! Definitely the sound of singing! But what an unusual voice.

He sat perfectly still, and listened.

And he heard it again:

> "Spinifex, yacka and mulga roots,
> Wallabies, lizards and bandicoots,
> Emus, goanna and white cockatoos,
> Redgums and dingoes and kangaroos . . ."

Spindles sat astonished. Here was a song about all his friends—and at least one of his enemies!

He looked around in the direction of the sound, but he couldn't see anyone at all. He stood up. He still couldn't see anyone.

Then, from right in front of him, it seemed, came a sparky, chirrupy voice: "G'day," it said. "How are you?"

Spindles looked down. The voice came from a small animal about the size of a rabbit. It had a long snout, with a pointy nose, whiskers, large ears, and hind legs like Joey's.

Its fur was reddish-brown, almost the same colour as the red earth on which he stood. And that is why he had been hard to see.

Spindles didn't know what to say. Finally he blurted out, "Who are you?"

"Well, you could say, 'Hello' first, young man. But since you asked, my name is Bilby, and I am a desert bandicoot. My biological title is *Genus Perameles* of the—"

"Desert bandicoot!" interrupted Spindles. "Really?"

"Of course," answered Bilby. "What else?

> "Biologists and scientists
> And scholars all agree,
> That desert bandicoots are rare,
> But not extinct, I do declare,
> As you can see by me!"

Spindles was delighted. Not only had he apparently found a desert bandicoot, but he had found a most entertaining one. For as he sang, Bilby danced around in a little circle on his hind legs, beating time with his front paws.

"Are you really a desert bandicoot, Bilby?" he asked.

"Sure am," answered Bilby. "Have you ever seen a coot as bandy as me?" And again, he jumped up and down in a kind of dance, laughing at his own joke.

"Then desert bandicoots are not extinct after all?"

"Would I be here if we were?" asked Bilby.

"I suppose not," replied Spindles. "I'm so glad. I've been hoping I'd find one."

"One what?" asked Bilby suspiciously.

"A desert bandicoot, of course."

"Oh." Bilby paused. "Why?"

"Well, it's Easter and my mum said that if I found a desert bandicoot she'd believe in the resurrection and then that would mean that—"

"Hang on, young fellow. You'll have to explain all that to me, I don't get it. But first of all, who are you anyway? You haven't even introduced yourself yet, you know."

So Spindles told Bilby all about himself and why he was so pleased to meet him.

"And now, if you will come home with me, I'll show you to my mum and everything will be all right," Spindles concluded.

"Hey, hold on a bit! Go home with you, Spindles? How stupid do you think I am? If you took me home I'd never get out alive. And Gloria wouldn't like that."

"Gloria? Who's Gloria?"

"My mate, of course. Who else?

The desert is a lonely place,
It's nice to know a friendly face,

> That first time that I saw-i-'er,
> I fell in love with Gloria."

"Is that the best you can do?" asked Spindles.

"No. But it'll pass for the moment."

"Anyway," Spindles went on, "why won't you come home with me?"

"I should think that would be obvious, Spindles. You know as well as I do that desert bandicoots are rare. There are a few of us left, but we've only survived because no one knows we're here, except for Lonely and you. And he's had enough sense to keep his mouth shut."

"Meaning I should do the same?"

"Naturally. If people find out we're here, the place will be swarming with visitors, and we'll be wiped out in no time. Leave well alone, I say."

"But how am I going to prove to my mother about the resurrection?"

"Well, now, that is a problem."

And Bilby sat down on his haunches to think. As he did so, he was suddenly joined by another bandicoot. It was obviously Gloria. She was very like Bilby, except that her eyelashes were longer, and her face a bit softer. Bilby greeted her with,

> "Here's my little friendly mate,
> She's running just a fraction late,

But since she's got some tasty roots,
(The ideal lunch for bandicoots),
I'll simply give a friendly smile,
And welcome her in royal style."

And with that, Bilby gave a lavish bow, and then stood straight until she was seated alongside of him.

"Spindles, meet Gloria. And Gloria, meet Spindles."

They both greeted each other and then again discussed Spindles' problem. As soon as Gloria found out all about it, she had an idea.

"Go and talk to Redgum about it," she said.

"Do you know Redgum, too?" asked Spindles in great surprise. "He's never told me."

"Of course not! He knows our secret, and he never tells anyone a secret, unless it's the right thing to do," answered Bilby.

And Spindles knew that he was right.

So, they all went up over the top of the hills and down the other side. Bilby and Gloria stayed hidden under some scrub while Spindles went down to talk to the great tree.

It didn't seem any surprise to Spindles that Redgum seemed to know what he wanted even before he got there. And so there were no other animals around at all—for even they didn't know about the bandicoots.

"You only have to tell your mother, don't you, Spindles?"

"Yes, Redgum."

"No one else has to see Bilby or Gloria?"

"No, Redgum."

"Well, why don't you take your two new friends to a place near the homestead, and ask your mother to come out by herself to see them?"

This was obvious, when you thought about it, and so this is what Spindles did.

He left Bilby and Gloria in a clump of mallee scrub about two hundred metres from the homestead. Then he went in to see his mother.

"Mum, there's something secret I want to show you. Will you promise never to tell if I do?"

"Why should I, Timothy?" his mother asked, rather amused at Spindles' secrecy.

"You'll see when I show you, Mum," he answered.

She could see no harm in this, so she agreed. They walked outside and approached the clump of trees. When they arrived, the two little animals crept slowly out.

"Good gracious!" said Spindles' mother. "What are they?"

"Desert bandicoots, Mum," said Spindles triumphantly.

"But wherever did you find them? Why not show them to Dad? And however did you get them to stay here? And why did you want me to see them?"

Spindles couldn't tell her about his conversation with the bandicoots, of course. That would have been too much. But he told her that they had been very tame and had seemed quite happy to stay where he put them. Naturally, he wouldn't say where he found them, and he insisted that they be let go.

His mother was very understanding, and agreed that it would be unwise for anyone to be told where they had come from.

"Now will you believe that Jesus rose from the dead, Mum?" Spindles asked.

"What do you mean, Timothy?" his mother answered. "What have desert bandicoots got to do with that?"

"Don't you remember, Mum? You said that if I showed you a desert bandicoot, you would believe—"

Spindles' mother interrupted him. "But Spindles, whether there are desert bandicoots or not, doesn't prove the resurrection."

"But you said—"

"Yes, I know I did. And I will say one thing. I didn't know it meant so much to you before. You really care about it."

"I do, Mum."

"Well, I promise you that I'll look into the subject again. Will that do?"

"Oh, yes, Mum. That'll be beaut."

Spindles' mother went back inside, and he took Bilby and Gloria back to the hills. By the time he returned, the sun was setting, and there was a golden glow along the ridges. There was no breeze now, and every leaf hung still and black against the paling sky. Spindles watched fascinated as the gold of the range tops changed slowly to mauve and then deepened to dark purple. He had seen it a thousand times, but he still loved it.

He just had time to visit Redgum before he turned for home.

"She still doesn't believe, Redgum," he said of his mother.

"Don't worry, son," said the great tree. "If she is really sincere (and she is your mother, isn't she?) she will find the truth. Jesus Christ said, 'Seek and you will find,' and this applies to your mother as much as to anyone else. If she really seeks him, she will find him. For he is the truth."

As Spindles rode home, he thanked God that Jesus was indeed risen from the dead, and alive forevermore.

And he thanked the Father that he could use even a desert bandicoot to make it known.

Author's Note:

Where *Spindles* Comes From, and Why

1. The stories' message. *The Spindles stories just "happened." At Christmas time, 1973, I searched in desperation for a story to tell at a Sunday School Christmas party. I had used up all my old Christmas stories—some of them already more than once. So as a last resort I decided to write my own.*

Half an hour later, with sketchy notes of what is now the first chapter of the book, I faced the children and launched forth. They liked it!

So I began the next story—and then the next. And here in this book are the first seven. In my opinion, the first is the worst, and the second the best, but you will have your own thoughts on that.

You will have noticed that each story has its own message, and that all the stories add up to a total message. You will also have noticed that the message is not "pushed." I wanted the stories still to be stories—not children's sermons. Furthermore, many truths are suggested which are not brought out openly at all (e.g., the need for Spindles to use his faith based on the Word, in the story of the flooded creek). You may want to draw these ideas out in using the stories: that is up to you.

Parents will find the stories good for bed-time reading etc. Teachers will find them useful as a kind of serial over several weeks or months of Sunday School gatherings etc.

If your children like them as much as my own children do, I shall be entirely satisfied. (My children may be biased!)

2. Biological and botanical content. *I have made every effort to see that all the biological and botanical matter is accurate. As far as I know, the trees, plants and animals are all accurately described. And—except for the fact that some of them talk and are shown in some of the pictures as wearing clothes—so too are their habits.*

Although I can find no record of an emu dying of snakebite (it is unlikely that it would be recorded anyway), both horses and sheep have been known to die in this way. And although the emu's legs are covered with thick, hard skin, it is quite possible that a snake's fangs could penetrate, especially if the emu were still. That an emu could race against a cyclist is quite feasible, and it has in fact been known to occur. And the story of the flooded creek is not an exaggeration. That's how it happens!

3. Authenticity. *It has been suggested that by hearing the gospel story as part of a fairy tale, some children will fail to distinguish reality from fantasy. I hope this is not so. I can only say that those children who have heard the stories so far seem to have had no difficulty.*

4. Appreciation. *Thanks to Lorraine Lewitzka for her delightful artwork; to Pamela Tough for her typing and to my wife and children for their excited encouragement. Spindles has become almost one of the family!*

Finally, let me say that I love the Lord and I love Australia. I guess that both of these loves are reflected in the stories of Spindles.

(Adelaide, S.A. 1973)

P.S. *Since I wrote the above comments in 1973, Spindles has become part of many, many families all over Australia and overseas! Several more books have appeared, and so, too have other products based on Spindles and his stories.*

The stories have been used as puppet plays, radio serials, children's plays, flannelgraph presentations and so on. There are literally tens of thousands of children and adults who have now enjoyed the adventures of Spindles and his friends.

Spindles is obviously here to stay! I somehow think that our Lord, who himself used stories to teach eternal truths, may have had more than a little to do with it, and I give the glory to him.

(Unley Park, S.A., February, 1981)

GLOSSARY

Aborigine, an original black Australian.
Alice Springs, the only large town in the centre of Australia.
Aussie, colloquial term for an Australian.
Ayers Rock, the world's largest monolithic rock, which stands in the centre of Australia. It is approximately three and a half kilometres long and two kilometres wide.

Bandicoot, a rabbit-sized mammal with a pointed nose. It basically feeds on roots and other vegetation.
Bearded dragon, a rather fierce-looking but actually small and harmless lizard, so called because of a large frill around its neck and its habit of opening its mouth wide in apparent anger.
Beaut, Australian slang for "very good" or "excellent."
Beauty, an expression which means something like "great!" or "terrific!"
Billy, a large can with a lid and handle, something like a paint can in shape and size, used for making tea over an open fire.
Boundary rider, a stockman whose particular task is to patrol the extensive fences of a sheep station. He usually rides either a horse or a motorcycle.
Bush, a wooded area or country land in general, especially in remote areas.
Black boy, another name for grass tree.

Correspondence School, a school for children in remote areas where lessons are conducted both over radio and by mail.

Crow, a black, scavenging bird with a mournful cry.

Darwin, the capital city of the Northern Territory, situated on the northern coast of Australia.

Dingo, a wild dog.

Dinkum, see *Fair dinkum.*

Dog fence, a huge, high fence about eight thousand kilometres long that prevents dingoes from entering sheep country.

Emu, a large non-flying bird something like an ostrich. Usually greyish-brown in color.

Fair dinkum, an expression which means something like "really" or "truly" or "on the level."

Flying Doctor, a medical service in the Outback that provides efficient and speedy assistance to people in remote areas.

Fossick, fossicking, to search or look for something.

Galah, a grey and white cockatoo with pink chest and feathers, and a noisy, high pitched cry.

Goanna, a large monitor lizard which can run fast and climb well.

Grass tree, an unusual bush with a thick stem and a crown of spiked foliage. Usually stunted in growth but can reach a height of five metres or so.

Joey, a young kangaroo, usually still being carried, at least some of the time, in its mother's pouch.

Kangaroo, a marsupial with large rear legs used for leaping, a heavy tail used for balancing and support, smaller forelegs, which are more like arms, and a smallish head. Most kangaroos are about a metre tall, but some reach nearly two metres.

Lizard, sleepy, a thick, slow-moving lizard about 25 centimetres long with a stumpy tail and a blue tongue. Also called stumpy-tailed or blue-tongued lizard.

Mallee, a scrub-like eucalyptus tree with several trunks, usually growing only to about five metres high.
Mulga, a form of acacia tree, scrubby and untidy. The word "mulga" is also used for a whole area of Outback country, whether there are mulga trees there or not.

Numbat, a termite-eating marsupial about the size of a large rat, which has a bushy tail and a striped back. The official mammal symbol of Western Australia.

Outback, the term used to describe the huge areas of desert and sheep and cattle country in the centre of Australia.

Piton, a spike used by rock climbers to secure their ropes.
Porcupine grass, a prickly grass with long, pointed leaves something like a porcupine's quills, which usually grows in clumps.

Redback spider, one of the two dangerous Australian spiders whose bite may be fatal. It is small, with a body about the size of a large pea and a red stripe down the back.
Redgum, a large eucalyptus tree which may grow to a height of fifty metres whose wood is a reddish-pink color internally but whose bark is grey or fawn.

Saltbush, a low, grey-green colored bush which grows in dry areas, especially dry saltpans.
Scree, an area of loose stones on the slope of a hill.
Scrub, another name for bush or low wooded country.
Shanghai, a slingshot.
Sleepy lizard, see Lizard, sleepy.
Spinifex, another name for porcupine grass.

Station, a large Australian sheep farm.
Station hand, a man who works on a station.
"Stone the crows," an expression, often of surprise.
Similar to "Son of a gun" or "How about that?"
Stockman, a man who works on a station,
especially in handling of sheep or cattle.
Sturt Pea, a native Australian plant which
grows close to the ground. It has grey-green
leaves, something like the leaves on a small
melon plant, and distinctive bright red and
black flowers. It is the South Australian floral
emblem.

Tasmania, the southernmost State of Australia,
which is actually an island.
Tasmanian devil, a small dog-like creature with a
fierce demeanor and a screeching cry.
Tasmanian tiger, a wolf-like creature with a
striped back, which is now probably extinct.
Torch, a flashlight.
Tussock grass, a form of grass which grows in
clumps or tussocks.

Ute, short for "utility."
Utility, a small truck. Called a pick-up truck in the
United States.

Wallaby, a small kangaroo.
Wedgetail eagle, a large eagle with a tail which has
a wedge shape.
Wild hops, a wild flower with bright pink flowers,
which was originally imported by Afghan camel
drivers as camel feed, but which is now very
widespread in some parts of the Outback.
Willy-willy, a small whirlwind or "dust devil."
Wombat, a marsupial that lives in a burrow. It is
something like a small bear, fairly slow-moving, and
usually quiet and withdrawn.

Yacka, a grass tree.